ECLAIRS
AND ECTOPLASM

LATTES AND LEVITATION - BOOK 4

CHRISTINE POPE

This is a work of fiction. Names, characters, places, and incidents are either the product of the author's imagination or are used fictitiously. Any resemblance to actual events, places, organizations, or persons, whether living or dead, is entirely coincidental.

ECLAIRS AND ECTOPLASM

Copyright © 2023 by Christine Pope

ISBN: 978-1-946435-64-4

Published by Dark Valentine Press

Cover design by Romancepremades.com.

Ebook formatting by Indie Author Services

Don't miss out on any of Christine's new releases—sign up for her newsletter today!

CHAPTER 1

Things That Go Bump

Leila Moreno, one of the girls who worked at the Plaza Hotel's bar down the street, came into Levitation Latte on a bright early June afternoon. Summer heat had descended with a vengeance, making me hope our monsoon storms would arrive sooner rather than later, since the rain and clouds always helped to moderate the temperatures a bit.

I was working at the coffee shop alone...and would be for the next two weeks, since my best friend Deanne—who also happened to be my one and only employee—was lucky enough to have in-laws who'd gifted her and her husband Mike with a surprise vacation in Hawaii in celebration of their fifth anniversary. The trip was made possible by an inheritance from one of Mike's great-aunts, who'd passed a few months earlier. While I was happy that the couple would be able to celebrate their anniversary in style...and also, if I wanted to admit it to myself, just the teeniest bit jealous, since I'd never been to Hawaii...I hoped these two weeks at Levitation Latte wouldn't be too crazy busy.

So far on that particular Monday, I'd had a steady stream of customers, but not so many that I hadn't been able to grab the opportunity to slip into the bathroom when I needed to, or to help myself to one of my ham and cheese croissants and sit down with it at one of the coffee shop's tables so I could take a quick lunch.

Actually, afternoons tended to be slower in the summer, just because I didn't get the usual influx of high school students dropping in to get a mochaccino and a muffin for a snack on their way home from school.

Leila generally came by around three or so, not too long before it was time for me to close up at three-thirty. Although the Plaza Hotel had its own coffee stand in the lobby, they didn't have iced green tea, which seemed to be her drink of choice when she needed the energy to make it through the rest of her shift at Byron T's, the hotel's bar.

"It's been crazy over there," she said as I handed over her grande green tea.

"Busy?" I asked. Early summer tended to be pretty lively for Las Vegas's hotels and tourist spots, although the same monsoon storms that I and the rest of the locals welcomed tended to put a damper on things...no pun intended...as summer wore on.

"Yes, but that's not the problem." Leila sipped some of her iced green tea before adding, "No, ol' Byron's really been acting up lately."

I couldn't help blinking at her comment. Byron T. Wells had owned the Plaza Hotel back in the early twentieth century, and it was widely rumored—actually, pretty well documented, to tell the truth—that he still hung around the place. I hadn't encountered his spirit, probably because I'd never stayed at the hotel, but plenty of other people had reported run-ins with him, or claimed that they'd smelled spectral cigar smoke in the third-floor hallway while going to and from their rooms. The hotel's bar, Byron T's, was named after him, although he wasn't supposed to be the only spirit that had taken up residence in the place. The spirits of a little boy and girl and an older man also lingered in the basement and lower level, near the old boiler room, and I had to admit I always got a creepy feeling when I went to use the public restroom down there, although I'd never actually seen anything.

"'Acting up'?" I repeated.

Another pull at her iced tea, and Leila said, "Knocking over things, opening doors. A woman on the third floor said she heard a man laughing outside her room, but when she looked into the hallway, no one was there. Freaked her out so much that she packed her bags and left right then, even though she was supposed to stay for another two days."

I had to admit all this sounded pretty creepy. However, Byron's ghost had been haunting the hotel for almost a hundred years, and in all that time, it didn't sound as if he'd done anything except make his presence known in ways that might have been disconcerting but definitely weren't dangerous.

Before I could say anything, Leila went on, "That's why I came over here today."

"I thought you were here for the iced tea."

She grinned. A couple of years younger than my own twenty-nine—she'd been two years behind me in high school—Leila was equally dark, with long near-black hair and big brown eyes, although her coloring came from ancestors who'd been in New Mexico for nearly four centuries, while mine had been inherited from my Italian mother.

A woman I'd done my best not to think about ever since she'd dropped unexpectedly into my life a few months ago after being absent from pretty much the moment I'd been born. Of course, this time she'd stuck around for an even shorter period, and had spent less than a week in town before she headed back to New York.

"No," Leila said, "I figured since you were Las

Vegas's one and only psychic, maybe you could go over to the hotel and check it out."

Danger, Will Robinson! flashed through my mind. The last thing I wanted right then was to deal with anything psychic or remotely supernatural. I might have inherited magic talents from both sides of my family, but I'd been doing my best to ignore all of it for the past couple of months and pretend I was as relentlessly normal as possible.

And I especially didn't want to think about the Petrucci magic. Honestly, if I could have figured out a way to have that particular "gift" surgically removed, I'd have done it in a heartbeat.

"I'm not psychic," I protested. "I just read tea leaves."

This denial of the O'Malley magic I'd gotten from my father's side of the family didn't seem to have much effect on Leila. She planted the hand that wasn't holding her iced tea on one hip and sent me a very direct look.

"Well, I'm pretty sure that if I tried to read tea leaves, all I'd see is a bunch of mushy chunks inside a cup," she said. "If you don't want to call them psychic powers, then whatever, but it still seems to me that you're the best person in Las Vegas to deal with a ghost."

Deep down, I knew she was right. Oh, sure, there was that one woman, Tituba Alcantar, who had a palm-reading shop down on the frontage road near the interstate, but all of the locals knew she wasn't actually a psychic. She seemed to mostly support herself by scamming money from travelers passing through town, although she also bartended at Blackie's—a local club/bar about a quarter-mile from her shop—when the tourist cash dried up during the winter.

Anyway, Leila knew Tituba was a scammer, so there wasn't much point in talking to her.

Whereas I....

There were probably plenty of people in town who didn't much believe in my gifts, but since I'd done a lot of accurate readings for neighbors and other residents, the word had gotten out that I generally was on the level. No one talked about these things in front of me—and I'd sworn Deanne and Mike and my friend Max to secrecy on the subject of my magical talents—and yet I guessed that I'd still been the topic of quite a bit of gossip as people tried to figure exactly how I'd been able to guess that Lucy Margolis was about to win the lottery, or that Dave Ortiz was about to be offered a job in Santa Fe making double what he'd been earning here in town.

No, all those incidents were exactly why Leila had come to see me.

I glanced up at the clock on the wall behind the counter. Ten minutes past three.

Trying not to sigh, I said, "I'll be there a little after three-thirty."

———

Because it was a Monday, Tilly—the alley cat who informally lived in the back of my coffee shop and whom I'd given the ability to talk more than six months earlier—was still out roaming downtown when I locked up the store and headed toward the Plaza Hotel. On weekends, she came home with me...most of the time...but during the week, she slept in the storeroom and slipped in and out via the cat door I'd installed for her a while back.

The sun baked down from overhead, and I was glad I only had to walk a block to get to my destination, although the historic downtown looked cheerful enough despite the heat, with the trees in Plaza Park green and providing lots of shade. I supposed it would have been a lot worse in the "other" Las Vegas, the much bigger city in Nevada, but the mid-nineties were still hot no matter how you looked at it.

Quite a few people crowded the tables and the bar itself inside Byron T's, but I saw almost at once that today Leila was working with Abby Anderson, another girl who'd gone to our same high school, so at least there'd be someone to cover for her if

Leila wanted to slip away with me to do some ghost-hunting.

Which seemed to be pretty much her plan. As soon as she saw me walk into the bar, she murmured something to Abby and came over to meet me.

"Thanks for doing this," she said, although I noticed she kept her voice pitched lower than normal, as if she wanted to make sure none of the customers—most of whom seemed to be tourists, since I didn't recognize any of them—couldn't overhear our conversation.

"I really don't know how much I'll be able to help," I replied, but Leila just shook her head.

"More than any of the rest of us could."

I didn't bother to contradict her, or to point out once again that I really wasn't a psychic or a medium, wasn't anyone with the ability to communicate with the dead.

Strictly speaking, saying I had no experience with ghosts would have been a lie. This past fall, when Tom Gallegos, our town's former mayor, was murdered, I'd held a séance at my friend Max's house to see if we could reach out to Tom and have him tell us who had killed him. However, I hadn't encountered Tom in the otherworldly place I'd conjured for our meeting, but my grandmother Maureen instead. She'd told me in no uncertain terms that speaking with the dead wasn't my talent and that I shouldn't try communicating with the departed ever again.

Because I'd never wanted to be a medium, it had been pretty easy for me to obey that particular command.

Was I disobeying my grandmother now by promising to help Leila?

A little shiver of worry went through me, although I tried to tell myself the situations weren't remotely similar. Leila and I wouldn't be holding a séance. No, I was just going with her to see if I could sense any weird vibes. And if Byron T. Wells' ghost was really hanging around the place and wanted to have a convo with me, again, that would be because he'd been the one to reach out, not vice versa.

By the time Leila and I reached the elevator, I'd convinced myself I wasn't violating the promise I'd made my grandmother Maureen. This was just a little scouting expedition, nothing more.

As usual, the elevator smelled of old wood and slightly musty carpet, even though I knew the entire hotel had been extensively refurbished about a decade earlier. It moved upward with a slight jerk, making me put a hand on the brass rail that had been installed at around waist height.

"Oh, it always does that," Leila assured me.

I had to take her word for it. The one and only time I'd gone to one of the hotel's upper floors, I'd taken the stairs. Why we hadn't done so now, I wasn't sure, although maybe Leila had thought I might still be a little overheated from my walk here and had decided to do this the easy way.

When we got out on the third floor, everything seemed quiet enough, even though this was the time of day when people would generally have been checking into their rooms. Sunlight streamed through the tall window at the end of the corridor, and generally, the hallway looked like one of the least haunted places I'd ever seen.

All of the rooms were named after famous movie personalities; the one directly opposite where we stood was the "Tommy Lee Jones" room. I couldn't tell whether it was unoccupied or whether the people renting it were out for the day, but either way, there didn't seem to be much sign of life in the immediate vicinity.

"Was this where the woman heard the laughter?" I asked, since Leila was glancing around us in all directions, clearly uneasy, and didn't look as though she planned to offer any further information.

"Yes," she said, and sent another of those furtive glances over her shoulder. "She said it was out here by the elevator."

"Well, maybe she heard someone laughing inside the elevator," I suggested. That definitely sounded like the most plausible explanation to me.

But Leila just shook her head. "No, it couldn't have been anyone in the elevator. We were having some trouble with it, and the elevator repair guy was here working on it, so it was grounded on the first floor."

So much for that idea. Even though I tried to tell myself the woman had probably just overheard a man laughing one floor down, an uneasy little shiver decided to walk its way down my spine.

What if she really had heard the disembodied voice of the man who'd once owned the Plaza Hotel?

Since I didn't know what else to do, I wandered partway down the corridor, moving toward the window. As I took those steps, that sensation of uneasiness only seemed to ratchet up further, my back tensing more the farther I walked.

Then it was as if I'd stepped into a pool of ice water. I gasped, and heard Leila say behind me, "What is it?"

"A cold spot," I replied, even as I told myself there could have been a perfectly rational explanation for the icy sensation I'd just experienced. Maybe the air conditioning vent was pointed at that one particular location.

That theory didn't seem right, though, if only because I could tell the A/C was laboring to keep the top floor of the building cooled down on this very hot day, and I'd felt almost warm when I walked out of the elevator. It wasn't until I reached this location that I felt an awful sensation of cold.

"That means there's really a ghost, right?" Leila said. She had the kind of complexion that couldn't really go pale, but I could tell she wasn't thrilled by this latest development.

"Supposedly," I responded. "I mean, I've read that there are cold spots in haunted places. But this is the first time I've ever dealt with anything like this."

And even though there didn't seem to be anything else happening where I stood, I hurried back over to her so I could stand safely next to my companion. Safety in numbers and all that.

"Is there anything else up here?" she asked next, her voice dropping to almost a whisper.

I paused. While all my instincts were telling me to hurry over to the elevator and get the hell out of there, I didn't want to act like a complete chicken. I needed to do something to reach out and see whether Byron T.—or any other spirits—were hanging around the place.

Problem was, I didn't know the best way to go about this. Yes, I'd led that séance all those months ago, but even then, I hadn't known what the heck I was doing. I'd read some articles online about reaching out to the spirit world and had hoped whatever innate gifts I had for reading tea leaves and dreaming true dreams would bridge my obvious knowledge gap.

And they had. Or at least, I'd been on the astral plane and had talked with the spirit of my dead grandmother, even though she wasn't the ghost I'd been trying to contact.

Maybe all I needed to do was let those same talents I'd been born with take over now.

"Give me a sec," I told Leila.

She nodded, teeth catching a little on her lower lip as she went silent, obviously waiting for me to do my thing...whatever that was.

Since it looked as though the two of us were going to be alone up here for at least a little while longer, I allowed myself to close my eyes and settle into the stillness of that upstairs hallway, to see what I could do to reach out and detect its vibrations.

And...I didn't feel a darn thing.

Sure, I thought I could feel the floor shudder ever so slightly as the elevator descended in response to a call from someone on one of the levels beneath us. I could even hear the faintest of cracks and pops overhead, probably from the old building expanding in the afternoon heat.

What I couldn't hear was Byron T.'s laughter, or even the slightest hint that anyone—or anything—other than us was up here.

Well, except for that cold spot. Would it still be

there if I gathered the nerve to walk back over to that place in the hallway and find out for myself?

I decided I really didn't need to know.

"There's nothing here," I said. "Or at least, I can't feel anything at all."

Leila crossed her arms. "You felt that cold spot a minute ago."

"I know," I replied. "But just because there's a cold spot doesn't mean there's a ghost in that exact location. It's more like...psychic residue of something being there once upon a time."

Even as I spoke, I wondered if I was getting the description right. Like a lot of other girls that age, I'd had sort of a fetish for ghost stories and supernatural nonfiction when I was in junior high and my first year of high school, so it had been a while since I'd read any texts on the subject.

However, what I was saying felt mostly correct.

"Well, there's something going on here," Leila told me. "I've heard the banging and knocking on the walls, too, even if I didn't hear Byron T. laughing up here."

Judging by the way she had her hands set on her hips and she stared straight at me, I could tell Leila wasn't about to back down from this. And that was fine. She'd obviously witnessed strange things here in the hotel, even if they weren't about to duplicate themselves for me.

"I'm not saying you didn't," I said calmly. "I'm

just saying that I'm not sensing anything myself. Like I said, I'm not the ghost-whisperer. This is way out of my league."

The elevator dinged then, and let out a man and woman who looked like they were in their late forties, both of them weighed down with a lot more luggage than you'd think a stay in Las Vegas, New Mexico, would require. Leila and I stepped out of their way, and then she headed over to the elevator.

"We might as well go back down," she told me as we walked. "Abby can only cover for me for so long, and happy hour is about to start."

Leila's expression told me she was more than a little disappointed at not experiencing anything supernatural, even if she wasn't going to give me any more grief over my failure as a medium. "I'm really sorry—" I began, but she just stepped inside the elevator car and held the door for me to join her.

"It's fine," she said. "I knew it was sort of a long shot. We have all kinds of ghost hunters come in here, and sometimes they find stuff, and sometimes they don't."

That sounded about par for the course. I was far from an expert on all things supernatural, but I'd be the first to admit the world of the spirits wasn't all that reliable.

Leila pressed the button for us to descend to

the first floor. An uncomfortable silence filled the car, mostly because I could tell she wasn't in the mood to listen to my apologies.

Some witch I was.

The elevator bell dinged again as we passed the second floor. We didn't stop, though, probably because most people staying on that floor would just use the stairs to get to the lobby.

Then the elevator jerked, and I grabbed the handrail. Leila's eyes met mine, wide and worried.

"I thought you said you had someone here to work on the elevator," I said.

"We did. He said he fixed it."

Another jerk, and then my stomach lurched as the car began to fall.

Holy crap.

"Oh, my God—" Leila began.

She didn't get any farther than that, though, because the car slammed into the ground. Because I'd been holding the handrail, I didn't fall, but she wasn't so lucky. She stumbled and landed hard on her knees, then put her hands against the patterned carpet of the elevator car's floor.

Dazedly, I wondered why we hadn't hit harder...and then realized we'd only dropped about fifteen feet or so. It was sufficient to yank the arm that had been hanging onto the handrail hard enough that it felt as though it was being pulled out of its socket, but definitely not a deep enough drop that we'd been turned into pancakes or something.

Leila pushed herself to her feet. "Are you okay?"

"I'm fine," I said. "How about you?"

"My knees are a little banged up, but I'll live."

She reached over and pushed the button for the door to open, even as I held my breath, wondering what I would do if it remained stuck.

Use your cell phone to call for help, my brain told me. *You've still got your purse on your shoulder.*

Which I did. Or rather, it had slid down to the crook of my elbow during the elevator's plummeting descent, but I still had it with me.

Luckily, those sorts of measures weren't necessary. The door opened serenely, as though nothing out of the ordinary had just occurred, and Leila and I made our escape.

She muttered that she was going to talk to the manager and let him know what had happened. I said that sounded like a good idea, and hurried out of the hotel.

I wanted to be as far away from there as possible...and I knew exactly where I wanted to go.

CHAPTER 2

Who You Gonna Call?

"That sounds rough," Max said, tone sympathetic as he leaned over to pour some more sangria into my glass.

"Well, we only dropped one floor," I replied. Now that I'd been able to put more space between myself and the admittedly terrifying incident, I realized Leila and I probably hadn't been in all that much danger. Sure, if the cable had broken—or whatever it was that had gone wrong with the elevator—when we were descending from the third floor, then we probably would have been banged up pretty badly.

As it was...well, I was just glad that Max Sullivan's home at Sunset Ridge had turned into such a sanctuary for me.

He shook his head as he set the pitcher down on the table. As soon as I'd called and asked if I could come over, he'd immediately said yes...and that he'd just put together a new batch of sangria.

If that wasn't a sign from God, I didn't know what was.

His own glass full, Max leaned against the back of the love seat where he sat. Because it was such a warm, sunny day, we were out on the second of his home's two patios, this one with the outdoor living room space and climbing vines on the pergola overhead shielding us from the worst of the sun's rays.

And I could only be thankful that the movie he'd been supposed to film starting the last week of April had been pushed back to the very end of June. Otherwise, he wouldn't have been here in my hour of need.

Still in the friend zone, unfortunately—I'd resigned myself to the sad truth that Max Sullivan and I would only ever be friends, and it was silly to think that one of the world's most famous movie stars would ever settle down with someone like me —but at least it seemed as though I was his best friend, if nothing more than that. I was over at Sunset Ridge at least a couple of times a week, whether to go horseback riding, or hiking, or just hanging out on the property's expansive grounds, like we were now.

It was still something to be Max's closest friend, and I told myself I needed to be happy about that.

"Well, I hope they get a different elevator company out to look at that thing and find out what went wrong," he said, then sipped some of his sangria. "It sure sounds like the people from the first one didn't know what they were doing."

"That's for sure," I agreed. "I have to believe they'll want to get it fixed as soon as possible. With it broken, the hotel isn't exactly ADA compliant."

Those sorts of things always stuck in my brain, probably because of all the hoops I'd had to jump through when I was reopening the coffee shop after I inherited it from my grandmother. The amount of paperwork involved in getting a business up and running could be kind of staggering.

"True." Max paused there and gave me a look that was almost sly, blue eyes piercing even under the shade of the pergola where we sat. As usual, he was casually dressed, in khaki shorts and a T-shirt from Bosque Brewery, a craft brew outfit that had several brewpubs scattered around New Mexico, but the laid-back attire couldn't hide the chiseled perfection of his features and the just slightly over-long but expertly cut sun-tinged hair. "So...you were up there ghost-hunting?"

"I wouldn't exactly call it 'ghost-hunting,'" I replied, knowing I sounded a little too prim. "I was just checking things out for Leila. She says the hotel has been kind of out of control the past week or so."

"'Checking things out'?" Max repeated, then continued before I could reply. "Like...reaching out and trying to get the vibe of the place?"

Since that had been almost exactly what I was doing at the Plaza Hotel, I didn't bother to contradict him. "There's nothing there," I said. "I mean, there was a cold spot up on the third floor, but that could have just been a glitch in the A/C or something."

"Or something," Max commented, the corners of his mouth twitching a little. No, it wasn't one of his full-blown smiles, the kind that could reach to the back of the world's biggest IMAX theaters, but still, I knew I wasn't completely immune to its charms.

I sipped some more of my sangria. Although Max's bodyguard Lou did most of the cooking at the ranch, Max himself mixed up the sangria, and obviously considered it a point of pride, claiming he'd been taught how to do it by one of his co-stars, a Spanish actor named Luis Becerra. It definitely tasted authentic to me, although I had to admit I wasn't exactly an expert.

"So...I thought you weren't going to do the ghost thing anymore after our séance last fall," he remarked.

"I wasn't," I said. "I mean, I'm not. This was just a one-off thing to help Leila. But since I didn't sense anything, there doesn't seem to be much point in pursuing it."

"What about the elevator?"

Now I lifted an eyebrow. "You're suggesting the ghosts did it?"

Max gazed back at me, expression placid. "I'm not suggesting anything in particular. I'm just saying the whole thing seems a little suspicious to me."

Well, considering we'd had to deal with three different murder cases in our sleepy little town over the past six months, I supposed I could see why he might think there was more going on here than met the eye. However, all those murders had been committed by regular human beings with absolutely nothing supernatural about them...not ghosts or spirits.

"It's an old building," I said lightly. "Things can go wrong."

"An old building that's been completely rehabbed," Max returned. "You know how careful the owners are."

Actually, I did. The same company owned the Plaza Hotel here in the heart of Las Vegas, The Castañeda--which was located down by the railroad tracks—and another hotel called La Posada way out in Winslow, Arizona. All three of the historic properties had been meticulously restored and refurbished before they were opened to the public, so I knew the chance of an accident like the one Leila and I had just suffered occurring at any of them was pretty low.

Low, but not zero.

"Well, obviously the elevator was having issues already, or they wouldn't have had a repair person on site to take a look at it," I said lightly. "As for the rest of what's going on there...well, I'm sure there's a completely rational explanation for the laughter that one woman heard or the strange knocking sounds."

Now Max grinned, a full-wattage smile that made me glad I'd already drunk a glass of sangria and therefore had some alcohol in my system to buffer its effects. "Considering everything you can do, Skye, I think it's kind of funny that you're so quick to say none of this can be supernatural."

True, Max had been a witness to me working magic—not just making Tilly talk, but also floating around my living room like an overgrown moth or something. He knew I was not your ordinary coffee shop owner...and a far cry from the girl next door I'd once been...and was probably thinking that a person who could do all those fantastic things should be the last person to be so dismissive of supernatural goings-on.

Honestly, it wasn't that I was being dismissive, more that, even while I knew magic was real, I also knew Occam's razor tended to apply in situations like these. No point in saying the banging on the wall was ghosts when it was much more likely just some plumbing that needed to be fixed.

"There's a difference between being able to work magic and thinking everything must be ghosts," I pointed out, and Max just shook his head.

"Maybe," he allowed. "But what are you going to do if this stuff keeps happening? Don't you think you should at least try to help?"

"Of course I will," I said, a little annoyed that he'd think I was capable of standing back and doing nothing while one of our town's biggest landmarks —and most successful businesses—was assailed by ghosts and God knows what else. "And if Leila comes back and asks me to try again, then I'll do what I can. All I'm saying is we should probably let the elevator repair people do their work first."

"Fair enough," Max replied amiably, and swallowed some sangria.

He guided the conversation away from the thorny subject after that, suggesting a day trip to Taos on Saturday, since Levitation Latte was closed on weekends and the weather promised to be gorgeous. We'd made a couple of side trips to Santa Fe over the past few months as the weather improved, and although it felt a little strange to be walking around in public with someone as famous as he was, I couldn't deny it was also fun to be the recipient of so many frankly envious stares from a lot of the women—and a few of the men—we passed on the street.

Of course, none of them could have known that Max and I were friends and nothing more.

I told him a day in Taos sounded fab, and he invited me to stay and have dinner that night. Just a casual invitation, one he'd made plenty of times before, so I didn't read anything into it.

Even if I really, really wanted to.

The next day, I saw a van pass by my shop, one with the logo of some elevator repair outfit from Albuquerque emblazoned on its side, so it looked as though the management at the Plaza had decided to hire someone new to deal with their problematic lift.

Probably a good idea.

Tuesdays were never all that busy at Levitation Latte, although the hot weather meant I had lots of requests for iced coffee and iced tea. There were a few holdouts who needed their shots of espresso no matter what the temperature might be outside, but they were definitely in the minority.

A little after two, I got a text from Deanne, one with a photo of her and Mike attached. They were at some kind of swim-up bar and holding fruity drinks with paper umbrellas stuck in them as they grinned at the camera.

Aloha! Drinking a mai-tai for you!

Don't be jealous, I told myself, even though it looked like a lot of fun...much more fun than cleaning out the knock box for the fourth time that day.

Besides, Deanne might be in Hawaii, but I'd had dinner with Max Sullivan the night before. I needed to keep reminding myself that life always had an upside if you knew where to look for it.

Then, about fifteen minutes before closing, a stranger walked into the shop.

I knew he was a stranger because I definitely would have recognized him if he'd ever been in my coffee shop before, mostly because he had an absolutely gorgeous head of dark red hair, the kind of shade I might have thought had come out of a bottle if he'd been female but which I guessed in his case was all natural. Add that red hair to boyishly handsome features and a tall, lanky form, and he was absolutely the kind of man who would turn heads pretty much wherever he went.

He was wearing a faded gray T-shirt with what I thought was the Loch Ness monster printed on it, cargo shorts, and hiking boots. Unlike a lot of redheads, he was sporting a light tan—not the kind of deep golden brown that Max always acquired in the summer, but enough to show off the muscles in his biceps and legs.

The stranger's eyes met mine, and I smiled, hoping that I hadn't been too obvious about the way I'd been staring at him as he walked in. "Welcome to Levitation Latte," I said, glad that at least my voice sounded normal enough. "What can I get you?"

His returning smile showed a hint of a dimple in one cheek. "Hi, there," he replied. "Are you Skye O'Malley?"

Wow, a Scottish accent to go along with that amazing red hair. It wasn't so thick that I couldn't understand what he was saying, just obvious enough to be utterly and completely charming.

"Yes, I'm Skye," I replied, even as I wondered how he knew who I was.

Then again, my name was mentioned enough in reviews of the coffee shop on Yelp that it wouldn't have been too hard for anyone to figure out who I was, especially since I was currently flying solo at Levitation Latte while Deanne was enjoying herself in Hawaii.

However, that theory was shot down the second he spoke again. "Leila over at the Plaza Hotel told me I should come talk to you."

"Oh?" I returned, knowing I sounded way too wary. Considering the reason why Leila had reached out to me the last time we'd been together,

I figured it was probably a good idea to be cautious.

The stranger smiled again, and stuck out a hand. "I'm Calum McRae," he said.

Although shaking hands with a customer wasn't the sort of thing I did on a regular basis, I went ahead and wrapped my fingers around his. He gave my hand a single, hearty pump, then let go.

"I'm a paranormal researcher," he went on. "This summer, I'm traveling around the Southwest, visiting haunted hotels and other sites."

This admission made me relax just a little bit. If Calum was some sort of ghost hunter, then he was probably here to talk to me about what had happened at the Plaza the day before, and not to start probing into my work with tea leaves and trying to find out whether Las Vegas had its own resident witch.

"Oh?" I said. "That sounds interesting."

"It is," he replied. "Although I suppose I should have come at a different time of year. I hadn't realized how bloody hot it would be here."

Despite an inner urge to caution that wouldn't quite go away, I couldn't help relaxing a little at this admission. "Yes, late spring or sometime in the fall might have been better."

His eyes twinkled. To go with his hair, they were a clear green, the kind that might look a little grayish in some kinds of light. "But I'll take an iced tea—and also thank you for the lovely air conditioning you have in here."

"Just part of the service," I told him, repressing the urge to smile again. There seemed to be something about Calum McRae that made me want to grin like an idiot.

But at least I wasn't so smitten that I didn't forget to fill a tumbler with ice cubes, then pour some black tea over them. I handed him the glass, and he thanked me.

"I didn't just come over here for some tea, though," he continued. "Leila said I should talk to you about what happened at the hotel yesterday afternoon."

I gave what I hoped was a casual shrug. "If you've already talked to her, then you probably know the whole story. I don't think there's much I can add."

"Oh, you'd be surprised," he replied. After a glance around the empty shop, he added, "Do you mind sitting down with me for a few minutes and having a talk?"

Part of me really did. The other part, however, was just fine with sitting with Calum for as long as possible and listening to that lovely accent.

"Okay," I said, trying not to sound too eager. "But if someone comes in, I'll need to take care of them."

"Absolutely," he replied. "I know you're at work."

Having hashed that out, he took his iced tea and sat down at one of the nearer tables. I got myself my own glass of iced tea and joined him, and sent a quick glance toward the front windows to make sure I wasn't about to get mobbed by a busload of tourists or something.

But everything looked quiet on that Tuesday afternoon, with most people indoors rather than trying to brave the near hundred-degree heat.

"So," Calum said after I'd taken a sip of iced tea, "Leila says you're kind of the town psychic."

Thanks, Leila, I thought. Clearly, she hadn't gotten the memo, or she would never have said something like that to a man who was pretty much a complete stranger.

Because Leila had already spilled the beans, I couldn't exactly deny what she'd said. On the other hand, that didn't mean I shouldn't attempt some damage control.

"'Psychic' is a little over the top," I said. "I read tea leaves. That's about it."

Calum's russet eyebrows lifted ever so slightly, but he didn't reply at once, and instead sipped some of his iced tea. "You read them extremely accurately, according to Leila. And she said you've solved some crimes around here, too. She made it sound like you're some kind of psychic detective."

Oh, boy. I liked Leila a lot, but her tendency to over-share had put me in an extremely difficult position.

"I helped figure out a couple of murders," I admitted. There wasn't much point in claiming I hadn't been involved at all, since enough people in town knew I was the one responsible for making sure those killers were all behind bars.

And okay, Justin Hale, the guy who'd killed his co-producer after she discovered the affair he'd been having with a much younger production assistant, was still awaiting trial, since he'd been arrested only a few months earlier, but I had no doubt he'd end up in prison facing a life sentence once a jury had a chance to weigh in on his crimes.

"I'd say that was pretty impressive," Calum remarked. The dimple flickered in his cheek again as he added, "I'm not trying to put you on the spot here. It just sounded like you were the best person to talk to about the hauntings at the Plaza Hotel."

About all I could do was lift my shoulders again. "I don't know about that," I said. "It's not like I work there. I've never stayed a night in the hotel or anything like that. You'd probably get better information from the people who spend a lot of time in the place."

"I talked to Leila," he said. "And that girl who works with her—Abby?"

I nodded.

"They both said they've felt a few odd things, but nothing consistent. I'm just curious about what you've experienced there?"

"Besides having the elevator break on me?" I inquired, and he grinned.

"Yes, besides that."

For a moment, I paused, wondering whether I should tell him the truth or whether I should just blow him off.

But he was awfully cute.

Those green eyes didn't seem to miss very much. I wouldn't allow myself to sigh, or he definitely would have noticed.

"It's...creepy down on the lower level where the restrooms are located," I told him. "I've never liked going down there."

Calum nodded. "Leila and Abby said the same thing. Anything else?"

"I felt a cold spot when Leila and I were up on the third floor yesterday."

"Do you remember exactly where?"

I had to stop and think about it, since that minor blip had been overshadowed by our little rollercoaster ride in the elevator immediately afterward. "I think it was in front of Room 310?"

For some reason, my response seemed to please him immensely. He settled against the back of his chair, the smile returning to his sculpted lips. "You know what's significant about Room 310?"

Not being a student of the history of the Plaza Hotel, I really didn't. "No."

"That room was Byron T. Wells' office," Calum told me. "It's been well-documented that a lot of the phenomena experienced on the third floor take place somewhere near there."

Well, that made some sense. I had to admit my knowledge of ghosts was pretty limited, but what I did know seemed to indicate it wasn't always about haunting the place where you'd died. Otherwise, hospitals and nursing homes would be mobbed by ghosts. Instead, the spirits of the departed often seemed inclined to loiter in spots that had some kind of meaning for them during their lives.

So, bearing that in mind, it didn't seem too strange to me that Byron T.'s chosen spot to hang out was the upstairs corridor where he presumably had spent a lot of time.

"The cold spot was Byron Wells?" I asked.

Calum rattled the ice in his glass as he appeared to ponder my question. After taking a sip of tea, he said, "Not necessarily his ghost itself. More like...a place where his energy was concentrated."

I didn't know whether that was better than having his ghost standing right there, or worse. What if some of that concentrated energy had stuck to me?

Apparently picking up on my unease, Calum said, "It's nothing to worry about. It's just energy.

A kind that's sometimes hard to measure, but it can't hurt you." He pushed his half-drunk glass of iced tea aside, adding, "Actually, I'm almost more interested in the way both you and the two women who work at the bar are so disturbed by the lower level of the hotel."

"'Do you experience feelings of dread in your basement or attic?'" I quipped. The movie had always been a comfortable old favorite of mine, and I wondered if he would pick up on the line even as I made the comment.

I should've known Calum would recognize a *Ghostbusters* quote right away, considering what he did for a living. A corner of his mouth lifted slightly, and he said, "Precisely. I think we should go check it out."

"'We'?" I repeated, not sure I liked the sound of that.

"Of course," he said. "You're a sensitive of some sort, that much is obvious." He leaned forward, green eyes bright, eager. "I want you to come ghost-hunting with me."

CHAPTER 3

Flowers in the Basement

I stared at Calum, wondering whether he was teasing me or if he really was deadly serious. "I don't know anything about ghost hunting."

"You don't have to," he replied, looking undaunted by my dubious response. "I'll handle the equipment. I just want to see whether whatever is in the hotel's basement will respond to the presence of someone with psychic gifts."

Was it worth the effort to protest once again that I wasn't psychic?

Probably not. I'd noticed how he'd said "psychic gifts," not that I was an out-and-out psychic. A subtle difference, but one I had a feeling he'd be willing to argue.

The thing was, I probably could reasonably claim I was psychic. No, I couldn't see into people's thoughts, but I had dreams that sometimes came true, or which provided valuable clues that contained information I normally would never have been able to access.

Except for Deanne and Mike and Max, no one knew about my dreams. Everyone else in town thought all my intuitions came from tea leaves, which wasn't the whole truth. I did read the leaves, and they'd helped me give advice to my friends and neighbors, but they definitely didn't provide the complete picture.

Trying to argue with Calum's plan seemed disingenuous, considering he didn't know the whole truth about me.

Still....

"I'm working," I pointed out.

"Only for the next fifteen minutes," he replied, wearing a smile that I guessed had opened quite a few doors for him. "I noticed the hours painted on your front window when I came in."

So much for that protest. "All right," I said. While I wasn't exactly thrilled at the prospect of wandering around the Plaza Hotel's basement, I had to admit that if I really was going to do something so sketchy, I might as well do it in the company of someone like Calum McRae.

Except....

"How do you know they'll even let us down there?" I asked. "That part of the hotel isn't open to the public."

"Oh, Leila said she'd let us in," Calum replied at once. "So that's covered."

I guessed it was. Since I couldn't think of any other roadblocks to throw his way, I decided I might as well give in. "Okay," I said. "I close the shop at three-thirty, but I'm usually here another fifteen minutes or so getting things tidied up. Is that all right?"

He didn't look too dismayed by that small delay. "It's fine," he assured me. "I'll wait for you in the hotel bar."

Having a drink? Somehow, I doubted it. Not that Calum gave the impression he abstained, but more because wandering around and looking for ghosts after you'd had a drink or two didn't seem like a very good idea.

"Then I'll come find you there," I said. "I'll try to be there around a quarter to four."

"Super. See you then."

He fished in his pocket and put a five-dollar bill on the table, presumably to pay for the iced tea.

"That's way too much—" I began, but he just shook his head.

"No worries," he said cheerfully. "See you in a bit."

He went out, and I stared in bemusement at the bill on the tabletop. Then I released a breath, took the money, and headed over to the cash register.

Because it had been so slow that afternoon, cleaning up the coffee shop didn't take as much time as it usually did. I had everything tidied and ready to go for the next day's customers in less than ten minutes, meaning I could be at the Plaza Hotel's bar sooner than I'd thought.

But since I didn't want Calum to think I'd rushed over there because I was just dying to see him, I took a couple of minutes in the bathroom to tidy my hair, refresh my lip gloss, and do my best to look presentable without seeming as though I was trying too hard. So far, he hadn't given any indication that he was interested in me beyond my supposed psychic talents. All the same, I figured it couldn't hurt to put my best face forward...so to speak.

Of course, that face felt as though it was going to melt off even during the short walk over to the hotel. We weren't supposed to hit 100 today, but it sure seemed as though this part of New Mexico was going to get awfully close.

But the interior of the hotel was blessedly cool, giving me a chance to recover myself a little as I walked through the lobby and headed into the bar. Sure enough, Calum was sitting at one of the tables by the window, which gave a great view of the park across the street. Because it was so hot, not many people were out, although I spied a few stalwart types using the shade provided by all the tall trees to take their dogs for a walk or even just sit down and get some fresh air.

As soon as I approached him, Calum stood up and hefted a messenger bag over one shoulder. Clearly, he wanted to get right to work, even though he had a half-finished iced tea—a twin to the one he'd left behind at my shop—sitting on the table in front of him.

"Leila told me we could go through the back," he said, and sure enough, she waved at us from behind the bar, expression cheerful.

Well, of course she was cheerful. She got to stay up here on the main floor where it was safe.

But since I'd agreed to this expedition, I only nodded and followed Calum past the bar—earning us some quizzical looks from its patrons, who were probably wondering why a couple of people who looked as though they were also customers were being allowed back there.

Maybe they'd ask, or maybe they wouldn't. Either way, I figured that was Leila's problem.

I had much bigger things to worry about.

There wasn't a huge space behind the bar; the actual kitchen was adjacent to the hotel's restaurant, across the lobby. Stacks of glassware sat on carts, and I spied a couple of stainless-steel worktables similar to the ones I had in my own kitchen at

Levitation Latte, but otherwise, there wasn't much equipment to see.

On the other side of the storage space was a door. Calum went straight to it, obviously having been told by Leila where he needed to go. After he opened it, though, he paused and sent me a questioning look.

"Ready?" he asked.

Since I'd already agreed to go down there with him, there wasn't much I could do except reply, "Sure."

He nodded, apparently satisfied even though I knew my tone hadn't been exactly eager. Too late to back out now, though, so I followed him through the door and down the dark, narrow steps beyond it.

I'd never been in this part of the hotel before, and I could see why. This space was completely utilitarian, with none of the careful restoration on display in the rest of the building. One forty-watt bulb did its best to illuminate the stairwell, but it was still a lot dimmer in there than I would have liked. Its dull glow revealed bare brick on one side, with an unstained wooden handrail the only concession to safety.

Probably, people didn't come down here all that much unless it was to service the hotel's HVAC system. I could hear it thrumming away in the background, straining to keep up with that early June day's above-average temperatures.

"The boilers used to be located down here," Calum told me. "But they were all removed when the hotel was restored and modern heating and A/C were installed. We're lower than the level where the restrooms are nowadays. Can you feel anything?"

Good question. We'd reached the bottom of the stairs, and stood in a large room with bare brick walls and a serviceable but not very attractive cement floor. Scars on that floor seemed to mark the spots where the boilers had probably once rested, and the ceiling was a maze of ductwork.

It all seemed very industrial, and not the kind of setting where you'd expect to find any ghosts.

"I don't know," I said. "I mean, it's not the sort of place where I'd really want to hang out, but...."

My words trailed off, because just as I was speaking, everything seemed to turn icy cold. It wasn't like walking through that cold spot on the third floor.

No, this time it felt as though the cold spot was moving through me.

I shivered, and Calum's green eyes fastened on me, intent.

"What is it?"

"I think there's something here," I replied, speaking in barely above a whisper.

At once, he reached in his messenger bag and pulled out a small handheld device, not much bigger than the remote for my TV. As soon as he switched it on, I could see the needle on the display move to the right, almost disappearing into the plastic case that surrounded it. At the same time, it emitted a sharp beep.

"What's that?" I asked.

"EMF meter," Calum said, gaze still fixed on the little gadget's screen. "It measures electromagnetic activity in a particular location. There's definitely something in this space, or it wouldn't have reacted like that."

His words only confirmed what my senses had already told me, but I could still feel the hairs on the back of my neck beginning to lift. "What now?" I asked.

"Try moving around," he suggested. "I'll follow, and we can see where the EMF readings are the strongest."

I didn't know whether I liked the sound of that —all my instincts were telling me to get the heck out of there and not come back—but I told myself Calum was right next to me and I wasn't in any danger.

At least, I hoped I wasn't.

Following his advice, I began to walk toward a door I'd spotted on the opposite side of the room from the stairwell. The closer I got, the less cold I felt.

"Needle's dropping," Calum said from behind me.

"It definitely doesn't feel as creepy over here," I told him.

While that was true, I still wanted to open that door and run for the reassurance of the bright sunlight and warm day I knew were waiting somewhere outside. But I'd promised to help out, so I told myself I'd stay down here and assist him in gathering his readings for as long as it took.

Well, unless some ghastly thing straight out of *Poltergeist* decided to manifest in the space. If that happened, I was running for the hills and not looking back.

"Can you go back to the spot where the boilers used to be?" Calum asked.

Damn it, I'd been afraid he was going to say something like that.

"Um...sure."

I walked back over to that creepy corner, icy tingles running down my back with greater and greater strength as I approached. Behind me, I could hear Calum's EMF meter beeping like crazy, so I knew it had to be picking up the same frequencies I was.

If I'd known it was going to be this chilly down here, I would have brought along a sweater. As it was, I started shivering like someone wearing a bikini at the North Pole.

"How—how long is this going to take?" I asked through chattering teeth.

"Not long," he said. "I know this is hard. Just give me another minute."

A minute? I had to hope I'd last that long.

He stuck the EMF meter back in his messenger bag and pulled out a small voice recorder, the sort of thing you might use for taking notes during a meeting or something. I assumed he'd turned it on, but I didn't hear anything.

That was probably a good thing.

But after a moment or two, he said, "Okay, I think that's enough. Let's head back upstairs."

This time, we went through the door, which opened on a carpeted corridor that led up to the place where the restrooms were located. It felt much better to be in a public space like this, but that same creepy sensation still crawled down my neck.

Calum must have guessed I still didn't feel as though we were back on safe ground, because he didn't stop, only kept going as he led me back to the bar and to the table where he'd been sitting some fifteen minutes earlier.

"Fancy a drink?" he asked.

After what I'd just experienced? Hell, yes.

Leila hurried over, obviously eager to find out

46

what we'd discovered. "Did you see anything?" she asked.

"See, no," Calum replied. "But there's definitely something down in the boiler room. Now I just have to figure out what it is. In the meantime, though, we thought we'd have some drinks."

He sent a questioning glance at me, and I said hastily, "A glass of chardonnay, please."

"Whatever brown ale you've got," Calum added.

"Sure," Leila said. If she was disappointed to be brushed off like this, she didn't show it. Or rather, since we hadn't seen anything gory, she was probably all right with waiting until we could gather more conclusive evidence.

While we were waiting for our drinks, Calum pulled out the little digital voice recorder and set it on the table. "Let's see if we got anything."

"What are you looking for?" I asked.

"EVP," he said, then explained, "Electronic voice phenomena. It's a way of picking up spirit voices."

Even though we were safely back in the bar and I could feel the bright sunlight beating on the window next to us, some more of those creepy crawlies decided to make their way down my back. "You mean talking to ghosts?"

"Not exactly," he said, then paused as Leila approached with our drinks. After thanking her, he returned his attention to me. "It's not like communicating with spirits the way a medium would. It's more like recording what the spirits are saying to themselves, or picking up whatever energy they're currently broadcasting."

Doing my best to ignore the icy sensation at the back of my neck, I picked up my glass of chardonnay and took a sip. Cool and friendly, it traced its way down my throat and generally made me feel much better about life.

At least until Calum pressed the Play button on the voice recorder.

The sounds coming out of it only sounded like static, but a kind of static way more ominous than you might get from a radio. I sent him a questioning look.

"Background noise," he said, then sipped from the ale Leila had gotten him. "That's the main criticism of these voice recorders, that they're too sensitive to RF interference. But it's really not that big a deal. You just have to train yourself to filter out the noise and hear what the spirits are trying to say."

I wasn't sure I wanted to know what they were attempting to tell us, but I figured if I'd had the guts to go down into that boiler room, then I should be brave enough to listen to the recording while sitting in this bright, sunny space.

So I nodded and did my best to concentrate on

the crackles and pops that were coming out of the tiny speaker.

Then I thought I heard it. Just a single word, but one that made a whole new set of chills run down my spine.

Help.

That one syllable was oddly attenuated, rising into a sharp pitch at the end that might have hurt my eardrums if it had been played at full volume. As it was, I shifted in my seat, glad to feel the reassuring solidity of the chair's back pressing against me. I swallowed some more chardonnay.

"I think it said 'help,'" I said.

Calum nodded. "That's what I heard, too."

"What does it mean?"

His shoulders lifted, although I got the impression that his current casual attitude was more for show than anything else. "It could mean a lot of things. The spirit could be asking for help crossing over, or it could be echoing something it said while it was still alive. Or it could be offering help to us, trying to assist us in identifying who it used to be. These sorts of things aren't always cut and dried."

"Have you ever helped a ghost do that?" I asked. "Cross over, I mean."

Now it was his turn to reach for his drink and have another swallow. "Not directly," he replied. "I'm not a medium, or a ghost-whisperer. I've observed a couple of times."

"And it really happens? A ghost really can be helped to move on to the next plane?"

For the first time, he smiled, and some of the tension that had tightened his shoulders visibly relaxed. "Oh, definitely. It's the best way to clear a haunted house."

I had to admit that knowing it was possible to help a spirit move on relaxed me a bit. "Is that what you want to do here?"

"No," he responded at once, his tone emphatic. "For one thing, I don't have that kind of gift. Also, no one at the hotel has asked me to help cleanse it or anything like that. I'm just here gathering data."

"Right," I said. "The whole paranormal research thing." I paused, wondering whether I should stop there. After all, I'd only met Calum less than an hour ago. It wouldn't exactly be polite to start inquiring whether he could support himself with that kind of career.

But once again, it seemed as though he'd picked up on what I was thinking, because he grinned and said, "I'm writing a book now, but I got my start with a podcast and then a YouTube channel and a Patreon page. It's enough to cover my travels and other business expenses."

Well, that made a lot of sense. Considering how good-looking he was, I had to believe he must have a lot of subscribers and supporters who weren't even that interested in the supernatural, but who watched his videos just so they could see him and listen to that awesome Scottish accent.

"Anyway," he went on, "if someone had asked me to come here and get rid of the ghosts, I would have brought a medium along." He stopped there, gaze growing speculative as he stared across the table at me. "Although it seems as though I might have found one right here in Las Vegas."

Blood rose in my cheeks, probably because it was extremely awkward to have him looking at me that way. "I already told you—I'm not a medium."

"Not a trained one," he agreed. "But it's obvious to me that you have some definite talents in that area."

For about the millionth time, I wished my grandmother was still alive. Not just because I missed her horribly, and having her gone meant I didn't have any family here in town, but also because I had so many questions I wanted to ask her. She didn't have the Sight, but her mother had —and presumably had passed it on to me—and now that I'd had a bit more experience with the supernatural, I had so many more questions I wanted to ask. Had my great-grandmother been a medium, or did she just have true dreams the way I did?

But Grandma Maureen had been gone for more than three years now, so I knew I'd just have to muddle along as best I could on my own.

"Well, I don't know about that," I said, "but since no one's asked you to cleanse the hotel, it's kind of a moot point."

"I suppose so," Calum said, then drank some more of his ale. "At least I have some pretty concrete proof that this hotel really is haunted, and that means it'll be included in my book."

"Are you only including the places where you've experienced something for yourself?" I asked. I supposed that made sense, even as it had me wondering what crazy things he'd seen while he was wandering around Arizona and New Mexico and Nevada.

He nodded. "Yes, that's the angle I'm using. There are tons of books out there about haunted places, but there aren't nearly as many where all the hauntings have been personally documented by the author."

Since I hadn't read any books about ghosts lately, I'd have to take his word for it. Still, it seemed kind of strange to me that Calum would be expending this much time and effort to produce a book when—from what he'd told me, anyway—he seemed to make most of his money from visual media, like his YouTube videos.

I made a comment to that effect, and he just smiled.

"Oh, I'm planning to do some videos on the most spectacular hauntings later on," he said. "But

I got a decent advance for the book, and one of the stipulations in the contract was that the book has to come out before I can post any videos covering the same hauntings."

"Because the publisher thinks your followers will run out and buy the book so they can have access to its exclusive content," I remarked. At least, that sounded like what they must have had in mind.

"Exactly," Calum replied, looking pleased that I'd figured it out. "And I've been talking it up on my channel, letting everyone know they can expect something special."

Well, if what we'd just experienced down in the hotel's basement was any indication, he probably had a decent stockpile of hair-raising stories. And if his YouTube followers were as engaged as they sounded, then he probably would sell a lot of books, even to people who weren't usually readers.

"I also want to thank you for helping me today," he continued.

I looked down at the glass of chardonnay I held. "Wasn't that why you bought me a drink?"

He grinned, amused crinkles showing at the corners of his eyes. "That's just a down payment on a thank-you. How about dinner?"

Although his expression was light enough, I could tell he was serious...and I also got the impression he wanted me to know this dinner wasn't just about thanking me for going down into that haunted basement with him.

Should I say yes? He was extremely cute, and it sure seemed as though we got along pretty well, even based on our short acquaintance.

As usual, though, my brain piped up and asked, *What about Max?*

What about him? I thought sourly. *He's been back in Las Vegas for almost nine months, and I'm just as firmly in the friend zone as I ever was.*

And it wasn't as if I hadn't gone out to dinner with someone other than Max during that time. True, the man in question was Justin Hale, who'd only asked me out to cover up the murder he'd just committed, but still.

Sidelining myself over a crush that just wouldn't die was stupid.

I took a breath, lifted my chin, and said, "Dinner would be great."

CHAPTER 4

Initial Impression

We settled on meeting at The Skillet at six-thirty after I'd explained to Calum that I had to get up really early for work during the week. He didn't seem put off by the arrangement, and told me he'd see me there.

Feeling a little dazed, I'd walked back to the coffee shop so I could get in my car and drive home, while Calum headed upstairs to the room he'd rented at the Plaza. He told me it gave him additional cred to be staying at the same haunted hotel he was investigating, and I supposed that made some sense.

All I knew is that I wouldn't have slept a wink if our situations were reversed.

Luckily, the big farmhouse-style home I'd inherited from my grandmother was free of ghosts, despite its hundred-plus years. After finally buying a new car a couple of months ago—courtesy of an unexpected windfall in the form of a hundred grand gifted to me by a murder victim's brother, who only escaped prison thanks to my sleuthing—I'd cleaned up the garage so I wouldn't have to leave my brand-new baby out in the driveway. It was another Subaru, mostly because I was used to that make of car and didn't see the need to get all crazy, except this time I was driving a new Crosstrek in a sky-blue shade I couldn't resist instead of a twenty-year-old hand-me-down I'd inherited from my grandmother.

As for the color of my new wheels, why not have Skye driving something sky-colored?

Because Calum and I would be going out for an extremely casual meal, I didn't bother to change out of the jeans and black sleeveless top I'd worn to work. If I'd smudged my clothes with flour or something else, then sure, I would have switched them out for something clean, but I'd survived my workday relatively unscathed. As it was, I settled for freshening my makeup and tidying my hair as best I could.

Those tasks didn't take me very long, though. I wondered whether I should text Deanne and tell her I was going out on a date, then decided against it. Better to let her know what was going on after I had some developments to report...*if* I had any developments to report, that is. For all I knew,

Calum was just trying to fill up his evenings while he was here in Las Vegas, and I'd seemed like his best prospect for some company.

Or maybe he was doing his best to butter me up and talk me into taking another trek into the hotel's basement. After all, we'd gotten some decent evidence that at least one spirit was lurking there, but we didn't know who they were or why they lingered in that particular spot. The common gossip seemed to indicate the spirits of a little boy and girl hung around down there, along with an older man. Even though I could tell something was there, I had no idea which of them had uttered the "help" Calum and I had both heard on his digital voice recorder.

It was possible that it had been something else entirely.

A shiver moved down my back, one that didn't have much to do with my home's air conditioning, since I tried to keep it set at around seventy-six or seventy-seven so I wouldn't have crazy-expensive electric bills. True, that hadn't been my first encounter with a spirit, but meeting up with something unidentified in an unfamiliar space was extremely different from having a chat with your grandmother while standing in a beautiful glade that had been conjured on the spectral plane.

However, none of the stories I'd heard about the supposed ghosts of the Plaza Hotel had ever even hinted they were malevolent in any way. No, people might hear laughter or voices, or smell Byron T.'s cigar smoke, but it wasn't as though the ghosts were locking guests out of their rooms or pushing them down the stairs.

What about messing with the elevator cables? my mind asked then.

I shivered again, and decided it was time to go. Logic told me there was no way a ghost could have had anything to do with the elevator's woes. Spirits were energy, nothing more, and couldn't interact with the physical plane in any real way.

Or at least, I sure hoped they couldn't.

I picked up my purse and headed outside. Because the sun wouldn't set for a couple more hours, the heat was intense, but I welcomed it. The brightness and the warmth that surrounded me as I walked down the porch steps and along the path leading to the detached garage were both happy reminders that I was far, far away from the Plaza Hotel's dark, haunted basement.

Hopefully, I wouldn't have to return there any time soon.

The Skillet wasn't super busy that Tuesday evening, just lively enough to reassure me that there were people all around and that I didn't have to worry about ghosts while I was there.

Also reassuring was the sight of Calum McRae, rising from his seat at one of the tables as soon as he spotted me coming in through the door.

"I guess you didn't have any trouble finding the place," I joked.

"No, I let my phone guide me," he said. "Since it wasn't that far from the hotel, I just walked."

I gave him a disbelieving look. "In this heat?"

"Sure," he replied. "Do you want to order?"

It had been hours since I snacked on that ham and cheese croissant for lunch, so I was definitely ready for something a little more substantial. "Sounds good."

Because the table he'd chosen wasn't too far from where we had to stand in line to place our orders, I slung my purse over one of the chairs, hoping that would be enough to signal anyone looking for a place to sit that the spot was already chosen. Under other circumstances, I might have kept it with me, if only to cover my half of the tab, but since Calum had said this was his treat, I figured I didn't have to worry about that.

Once we were in line, I ventured, "I thought this kind of weather wasn't the sort of thing someone from Scotland would be used to."

"Oh, it's not," he replied, still looking cheerful...

and not at all sweaty from his walk over here. "But my family moved from Scotland to Southern California when I was in high school, so I've had time to get used to temperatures above fifty degrees."

Well, that helped explain why his accent, while definitely still there, wasn't so strong that I couldn't understand half of what he was saying, something I'd sometimes experienced when dealing with tourists from the U.K.

"What part of California?" I asked.

Now he appeared almost embarrassed. "A place called Brentwood."

I didn't know a lot about Southern California, but I vaguely remembered reading somewhere that Brentwood wasn't too far from Beverly Hills, and definitely wasn't low-rent by any stretch of the imagination. "Isn't that kind of close to the ocean? I didn't think it got too hot in the parts of California that are near the beach."

Once again, his expression was sheepish. "Well, my parents had a house in Palm Springs, too."

What, was Calum some kind of trust fund kid? I supposed that might explain why he had the money to travel wherever he liked and fund his YouTube channel.

Either way, it really wasn't any of my business.

Because I could tell he wanted to downplay his family's wealth—if that's even what was going on here—I just said lightly, "Well, if you spent time in Palm Springs, then I can see how the weather here in the summer wouldn't be a big deal."

He grinned, his stance relaxing a little. "Yes, this doesn't feel like much compared to 115 degrees."

By that point, we'd reached the counter, and it was time to put in our orders. Once again, Calum got a beer, while I asked for a glass of wine to accompany my burger. He opted for a taco plate, and a few minutes later, we were back at our table, with a number to set down there so the server would know where to locate us.

"To finding some ghosts," Calum said, and lifted his glass.

I didn't know whether I was as cheerful about that particular prospect as he was, but I went ahead and clinked my glass against his. "'To finding some ghosts,'" I echoed.

We both drank, and then he said, "Would you be willing to go back down there tomorrow afternoon?"

Making a return visit to the basement was about the last thing I wanted to do, but I only shrugged and said, half-joking, "I don't know. I guess it depends on whether I get another dinner out of it."

He chuckled, although his green eyes were serious enough as he met my gaze. "Skye, I would've asked you out to dinner again whether or not you went ghost hunting with me."

For a second, I could only stare back at him. It sure looked to me like Calum was sending me a pretty clear signal...and I didn't know quite what to do about it.

But because I didn't want the moment to grow too awkward, I said quickly, "I suppose I can go back to the basement with you. It'll have to wait until I'm off work, though."

He blinked, and the moment was gone. "Oh, that's fine," he said. "I was going explore the area tomorrow, check out some local history. And I need to write up my notes."

Those activities sounded as though they would be enough to keep him busy for most of the day. "Then it's a plan," I replied. My tone was cheery enough, but I couldn't ignore the ripple of unease that went through me at the thought of going back down to that haunted basement. Today had been scary enough.

What might we encounter tomorrow?

I had to put that question aside for now, though, because the server—a guy a couple of years younger than me named Tyler—came by with Calum's and my meals. We were quiet for a few minutes as we dug into our food, a silence broken after he finished one of his tacos.

"I really appreciate you doing this for me," he

said, now sounding almost diffident. "The two of us working together can accomplish a lot more than me trying to do all this on my own."

"It's nothing," I told him, even if that wasn't exactly the truth. While I was glad to help him out, I really, really didn't want to go back in that basement.

"No, it's definitely something," he countered. "Having someone with your gifts there amplifies the experience in ways I can't begin to explain."

That comment made me set down my burger. "Do you always work with psychics?"

Calum shook his head. "Not usually. I mean, a lot of the time, it's hard enough to get access to the places I need to see. If I went around advertising that I needed a psychic to help me, I'd probably have all kinds of fakes crawling out of the wood-work." He paused there, expression turning half rueful, half amused. "And I know that because the first time I was really serious about documenting a haunting, I asked on a local bulletin board whether there were any mediums or psychics who might be willing to lend a hand. You wouldn't believe the weirdos who surfaced, all hoping to get a moment of fame...and a paycheck."

"Oh, I think I would," I said, remembering all those supposed witches on YouTube I'd discovered when I was trying to figure out a way to harness my talents. Most of them looked as though they'd be all too willing to lie about their magical talents in order to make a quick buck.

Or maybe I was being way too judgmental. I didn't know anything about those women, but I had to believe only a fraction of them had real magical talents, if any at all. When my mother, Alicia Petrucci, had surfaced back in February, she'd made it sound as if having magical gifts was very rare, something that almost always ran in families. I didn't find that too strange, since my talent for reading tea leaves and having true dreams had come to me from my great-grandmother on the O'Malley side, and it just made sense for that kind of thing to be hereditary.

Of course, the magic on the Petrucci side was entirely different, and was much more centered on affecting the physical world. To be honest, it scared me a lot more than my O'Malley talents, just because I didn't know exactly how much trouble I could get in with magic that allowed me to make cats talk or fly around the house. After Alicia left—and left for good, because she'd warned me that her side of the family would come in search of me if they ever discovered my existence—I'd vowed never to use those powers again...or at least, not to use them in any way that would attract attention.

That was why I occasionally used my magic to levitate so I could reach something on a tall shelf, or to grab an ingredient I needed from the coffee shop's kitchen when I was almost a mile away at my house, but otherwise, I did my best to pretend those strange talents of mine didn't exist.

Anyway, what Calum was asking of me had nothing to do with the Petrucci magic I'd inherited. No, anything that dealt with the world of the spirits was much more an O'Malley thing...even if my grandmother had told me I shouldn't be messing around with that kind of stuff.

Looking much more relaxed now, Calum sent me a quick smile before reaching for another of the tacos that sat on his plate. "Anyway," he said, "I wouldn't have even come in to see you if Leila hadn't suggested it. I'd thought maybe she was exaggerating, but it sure looks to me like you're the real deal."

A flush touched my cheeks, one I hoped he wouldn't notice. Luckily, The Skillet wasn't exactly the most brightly lit restaurant in the world. "Well, a lot of this is sort of outside my scope, but I'll do what I can."

He didn't seem put off by that self-deprecating remark, although, since he abruptly switched the topic and instead asked me about any places I could recommend that he visit, he obviously could tell I didn't want to keep talking about my psychic gifts.

Whatever they were.

After dinner, he walked me to my car. By that point, the sun had dipped behind the Sangre de

Cristo mountains to the west, although true sunset was still more than an hour away. The temperature didn't seem as if it had dropped much, although a little canyon breeze made its way down the street and offered some relief from the heat.

"Thanks for dinner," I said.

"No, thank you," Calum responded at once. "For going along with me today...and for saying you'll do it tomorrow, too."

Once again, I questioned the wisdom of that particular decision, but it was too late to back out now. Besides, I'd survived that one foray, and there was no reason to believe I wouldn't survive another one.

At least this next time I'd know what to expect.

I shrugged, and then we gazed at each other for a moment.

Was he going to kiss me? This was a pretty public place, and even though the sidewalks were deserted for the moment, I supposed anyone could come along at any time.

Apparently, Calum was thinking the same thing...or maybe he'd never intended for us to share a kiss on this extremely informal first date.

"See you tomorrow," he said.

"See you then," I replied.

He lifted his hand in a half-wave, then turned and headed back toward the hotel. You couldn't see it from where we'd been standing, but I knew it was there, already shrouded in the shadow from the mountain, hiding its own secrets.

I supposed we'd just have to see whether we unearthed any of those secrets tomorrow.

That was probably one of the most excruciatingly slow Wednesdays I'd ever experienced at work, but eventually the time wound down to three-thirty, and it was time to close up shop and walk over to the Plaza Hotel, where Calum would be waiting for me in his room. The weather wasn't quite as hot as it had been the day before, mostly because monsoon clouds had clustered above, blocking the sun and promising some rock-and-rolling thunder and lightning in the not-too-distant future.

I wasn't sure how I felt about that particular prospect. Most of the time, I welcomed the monsoon storms and the relief they provided from the heat, but having a major thunderstorm going on overhead while wandering around a haunted basement didn't sound like a whole lot of fun.

But I'd promised Calum I'd help him today, and I'd never been one to go back on a promise. Who knows? Maybe we'd get down there and find absolutely nothing. I didn't know a whole lot about ghosts, but they definitely didn't seem like the most consistent entities in the world.

Calum answered the door as soon as I knocked, telling me he'd been anticipating my arrival. Today he looked just the tiniest bit sunburnt, as if whatever he'd been doing before I got here, it had involved being outside for a decent chunk of time.

"Ready?" he asked, and I nodded.

"Sure. Let's see what else we can find."

He must have let Leila know we were planning a return trip to the basement today, because she sort of smiled and waved as we came into the bar, then said, "Go on down," as if it was the most natural thing in the world to have a couple of amateur ghost hunters wandering around in the hotel's bowels.

But because she'd looked so relaxed about the whole thing, I didn't feel quite as tense as I had the day before as we started down the dim stairwell that led to the basement. In fact, I didn't experience a single creepy-crawly sensation, although I didn't know if that was because the ghosts had decamped for the day, or whether I was just feeling bolder because I'd already survived one of these forays.

Either way, I followed Calum into the basement without flinching, and thought maybe this ghost-hunting thing might be survivable after all.

He was wearing the slightest frown, as though he'd also noticed a shift in the basement's atmosphere, even if he couldn't quite identify what it was. A pause as he fished through his messenger bag, and then he brought out the little EMF meter.

His frown only deepened as he stared down at it. "I'm not getting any readings at all."

"Seriously?"

"Come look for yourself."

Obediently, I came over and stood next to him so I could look at the gadget. Sure enough, the needle seemed to be stuck over to the left and didn't appear inclined to move even the teeniest bit.

"So...the ghosts are gone?" I asked. No wonder I hadn't been feeling nearly as freaked out today.

"I'm not sure," Calum replied. "I mean, I doubt they're gone, gone. Once spirits settle on a place to inhabit, they tend to stay put. But they sometimes phase in and out, for lack of a better way to explain it. That's why hauntings can be so hard to pin down."

Trying not to sound too hopeful, I inquired, "Does that mean we're done for today?"

I should have known it wouldn't be that easy. "No," he responded immediately. "I want to poke around a bit. I was doing some digging in the local archives, and it sounds like there was a boiler explosion down here in the early 1920s. That could have been what killed our ghosts."

A boiler explosion? I looked around the basement, wishing the lighting was better so I could see more details on the floors and walls.

"Over here," Calum said, and headed over to the brick wall that formed the outer perimeter of the space. He laid a hand on the uneven surface. "See here? It's a pretty obvious patch. I think the explosion must have knocked out part of the wall, and this is the place where it was repaired."

I came closer. Yes, there was definitely a spot about seven feet across where the bricks were a slightly different size and shape from the ones that made up the rest of the wall. "A boiler could do that?"

"If it built up enough pressure. Those things can be like a bomb going off. They're lucky the whole building didn't cave in."

Yikes. Not being familiar with boilers or their explosive capabilities, I had to take Calum's word for it. "Where did you hear about the boiler explosion?"

"I went over to the library after lunch today," he replied. "They actually have a good little local history section there. I found an old self-published book by a man named Al Torres, who wrote about the town in the 1920s and '30s. That's where I read about the incident here at the hotel."

Well, at least the damage hadn't been so extensive that the hotel would have been a complete loss.

The building was such a landmark, I couldn't imagine Las Vegas without it.

"Any mention of anyone getting hurt in the explosion?" I asked next. That did seem to be the most logical explanation for the origin of spirits who lingered here. True, ghosts didn't always hang around the place where they died, but if the basement had been significant to them for some other reason, then that might have provided enough of a reason for them to still be here.

Calum hitched up his messenger bag, which was heavily loaded enough that it had begun to slide off his shoulder. "Nothing that I could find. But it was only one book. Now that I have a better idea of when it happened, it'll help me narrow down my search. And I wanted to take a closer look here."

I glanced around the space. The patch in the brick was so obvious to me now, I couldn't believe I hadn't noticed it when we came down here yesterday.

Then again, I'd been a lot more preoccupied with the creepy sensations I was experiencing and the way Calum's EMF meter had gone haywire.

But the device seemed quiescent for now, so I figured this was a very good time to do some exploring. "Well, you take this wall, and I'll take that one," I suggested, pointing at the plaster expanse a few yards away. It looked newer than the brick walls that formed the perimeter of the basement, but that didn't mean much. Since the hotel had been built in 1880, even a wall added in the early years of the twentieth century would have been decades newer than the original construction.

Calum seemed amenable to that plan, and dug a small Maglite out of his messenger bag and gave it to me. "That should help you see more detail," he said. "The lighting in here isn't very good."

No, it wasn't. I gratefully accepted the flashlight and headed over to the wall I wanted to inspect more closely, while he produced another flashlight and began shining it over the surface of the brick wall with the patch in it.

The whole time, I halfway expected that awful shivery sensation to start somewhere on the back of my neck, but it really did seem as though the EMF meter was right and the ghosts had taken a powder for the time being. Why now, I didn't know, but I figured I should be happy that I could conduct this part of the investigation without worrying about turning around and having a creepy ghost child, like one of those twins from *The Shining*, staring back at me.

To be honest, the wall I'd chosen to inspect didn't look very interesting. The plaster had dark patches, probably from long-ago leaks, but its surface was uniform enough. Maybe a scratch here and there and the occasional dark mark where something had been dragged across it, which I supposed was to be expected after standing there for the past century.

Except....

I leaned in and shone the light directly on the wall. What I'd thought were random scratches down near the floor didn't look quite so random when viewed up close.

"Hey, Calum!" I called out. "I think I might have found something."

He immediately turned away from the wall he'd been inspecting and came over so he could add his flashlight's illumination to mine. "Are those letters?"

"I think so," I said. They were small, barely half an inch high, so it wasn't too surprising that no one might have noticed them before now. "It looks like an 'A' and an 'M.'"

Because he was so much taller than me, Calum had to squat down to take a closer look. Eyes narrowed, he studied the spot in question, and then nodded. "You're right. Definitely 'A.M.'"

"Someone's initials?" I asked.

"Could be. I can't think of what else those letters might stand for."

Well, except as an abbreviation for the morning, which didn't make much sense. Whereas people were always leaving little scratches and abbreviations behind to mark a place they'd visited.

He pulled a black iPhone out of his messenger bag and took a few quick snaps of the initials, then returned the phone to the bag. "I'll see if I can find any records of the people who worked at the hotel back then. Maybe one of them left his initials here." His eyes lit up, and he added, "Maybe these are the initials of one of our ghosts."

That sounded like kind of a long shot. After all, how many hundreds of people had come and gone in this basement during the decades the hotel had been in operation?

But it was more of a clue than we'd had five minutes ago, so I told myself we should be grateful we'd found this much.

"Could be," I said, and straightened up. Kneeling down like that on a hard surface for too long always made my knees ache.

Face still way too cheerful for that gloomy base-ment, Calum brought out the digital voice recorder he'd used the day before to capture that one creepy EVP. "I don't know if I'm going to get anything today," he told me, "since it seems as if the ghosts are being pretty quiet for now. But I figure it couldn't hurt. Mind waiting a bit while I record for a couple of minutes?"

Honestly, I just wanted to get the heck out of there now that we'd found our one piece of possibly relevant information. But since I didn't want to sound like a scaredy-cat, I replied, "Sure. Go ahead and record however much you need."

He sent me a grateful smile and pushed the Record button on the device, while I just stood there and tried not to breathe too loudly so it wouldn't interfere with whatever it was trying to capture. After a minute or so of this, Calum was apparently satisfied with what he'd gotten, because he shut off the machine and put it back in the bag with the rest of his gadgets.

"All right," he said. "Let's go."

CHAPTER 5

Ships That Pass in the Night

"It's early," Calum said as we emerged from the basement. "How about we drive to Santa Fe for dinner?"

For a second, I could only stare at him. "You want to take a three-hour round trip to get something to eat?"

He shrugged. "Do you have a better idea?"

The sensible part of me wanted to say yes, I had a better idea. We could go to Charlie's for dinner, or to Smokin' Joe's, the new smokehouse-style restaurant that had opened down Bridge Street only a month earlier. Heck, we could even eat right in the hotel at its restaurant. That way, we'd stay here in town, and I wouldn't have to worry about getting back in time to go to bed at a decent hour.

But there was something enticing about the idea of heading over to Santa Fe, not the least of which was the utter anonymity of going to a town where no one knew me, and where there wasn't any chance of someone in my circle seeing me out to dinner with a handsome stranger and asking awkward questions.

"Okay," I said. "Let's go to Santa Fe."

The drive could have been awkward but wasn't, mostly because Calum regaled me the whole time with stories of his ghost adventures in the Southwest—whether it was the spirit of a former saloon girl supposedly hiding his jeans when he stayed in Tombstone for a few days, or hearing ghostly gunshots in the alley behind a hotel in Jerome, Arizona. And I opened up about the role tea leaves and dreams had played in solving the three murders that had taken place in my own hometown over the past year, a little surprised at myself for being so honest about everything that had happened.

"You're definitely psychic," Calum said as he maneuvered his '70s-vintage Land Rover into a parking garage in downtown Santa Fe. The vehicle had been expertly restored, and I guessed it had probably cost a lot more than a brand-new SUV might have. "You can call it whatever you want, but no one without psychic gifts would have been able to do what you've done."

"I don't read minds, though," I argued, and he only shrugged.

"There are lots of different ways of being psychic," he said, and put the vehicle in park. "Sure, telepathy is part of it, but there's also psychometry, reading auras, seeing the future in dreams, like you do. It's not one size fits all."

No, I supposed it wasn't. Still....

"It's not even like I see the future, exactly," I said. "Sometimes I see scenes from the past, and a lot of the time, my dreams don't even make sense to me until days later."

"Well, it's not science," he replied reasonably. "You can't expect your kind of gift to be the sort of thing that can be measured and quantified. Anyway, what're you in the mood for?"

"Any place we can get a table," I replied with a grin. "It's a Wednesday, so things shouldn't be as packed as if we'd come here on a weekend, but downtown Santa Fe can be crazy busy during the summer."

Calum didn't look too perturbed by our prospects. "Then we'll just wander until we find a place that'll take us in."

That sounded like as good a plan as any, so I went ahead and climbed out of the Land Rover. We'd left Las Vegas as soon as we'd decided on this jaunt to Santa Fe, meaning it was still pretty early, not even six o'clock yet. Because of the hour, I hoped we'd have better luck getting in somewhere than we would have if we'd been attempting to find a table at seven or even later.

The two of us headed out of the parking garage and wandered down San Francisco Street for a bit. It was very warm here in Santa Fe as well, although a couple of degrees cooler than Las Vegas had been. However, the monsoon clouds that had been threatening my hometown hadn't made it here yet, telling me this was a great evening for dining *al fresco*.

"Oh, I know where we should go," I told Calum as we paused at the corner of Galisteo Street. "The next street down, there's a rooftop restaurant and bar called the Coyote Cantina. They have great sangria, if you're into that kind of thing."

"Even if I'm not, a rooftop cantina sounds great. Lead on."

Glad that we now had a destination, I turned down Galisteo, then hung a left on Water Street, with Calum gamely keeping pace next to me. And sure, the cantina was crowded when we got there, but our luck held and a table emptied just as we approached the hostess station. A couple of minutes later, we were seated at a table for two and putting in our requests for drinks.

In fact, he surprised me by ordering sangria as well. "Thought I might want to blend in with the natives," he said with a wink, while I could only roll my eyes in response.

However, that didn't stop me from touching my glass to his after the waitress brought our drinks and saying, "Here's to finding out who 'A.M.' is."

"I'll definitely drink to that," he replied. "It might turn out to be nothing at all, but I can't help feeling like whoever scratched those initials into the wall is somehow connected to the hotel's ghosts."

I'd had the same feeling as well, even while I told myself it could be wishful thinking and nothing more.

"In the meantime," Calum went on, "I'll keep trying to look up more local history wherever I can, see if there's something else that might point me in the right direction. And I'll have a listen to that latest recording I made once we get back to Las Vegas."

"You really think there'll be anything on there?" I asked. "I mean, the ghosts seemed like they weren't even around today."

"It's possible," he replied, not looking at all dismayed that he might have recorded a couple of minutes of absolutely nothing. "Just because we couldn't sense the spirits doesn't mean they weren't there. They might have decided to lie low, but that doesn't necessarily imply they were gone altogether."

I didn't know what was creepier...actually

being able to sense the ghosts' presences, or having them around and not realizing it.

Neither option was very appealing.

Before I could say anything in reply, though, I heard an incredulous-sounding Max Sullivan say, "Skye?"

Shock coursed through me, but I forced myself to turn slightly in my seat and look up at Max. The cantina was crowded enough that he was practically brushing against our table, and a tight-faced woman who looked like she might be in her middle forties stood at his elbow.

"Oh, hi, Max," I said, doing my best to sound as casual as though we'd bumped into each other at Walmart. "What're you doing here in Santa Fe?"

"Margaret—my agent," he added, with a nod toward the woman who stood next to him, "was here for a meeting about an upcoming film festival, so I came down for the day to see her. Who's this?" he asked, gaze moving toward Calum, who'd been watching the exchange with some interest.

"Oh, sorry," I said, knowing I probably should have made the introductions as soon as I realized that was Max standing at my table. "Max, this is Calum McRae. He's been doing some research in Las Vegas. Calum, this is my friend Max Sullivan."

"I kind of recognized him," Calum said with a grin. However, he did stand up and extend a hand.

Maybe Max's eyes narrowed just the slightest

bit...or maybe I was imagining things, because the smile he wore was genial enough as he took Calum's hand and shook it. "Nice to meet you." A pause as he introduced Margaret to both of us. She didn't look too thrilled by this encounter and definitely wore the expression of a woman who wanted to be anywhere else. Then Max said, "What kind of research are you doing in Las Vegas?"

"Hauntings," Calum said promptly. "Skye and I have been having a poke at the Plaza Hotel."

"Skye and you?" Max repeated. Judging by the way his gaze slid toward me and one eyebrow lifted ever so slightly, I knew I'd have some explaining to do once the two of us were alone.

I shot a warning glance at Calum. True, Max knew all about my supposed magical talents—a lot more than Calum, actually, since of course I hadn't uttered a word about the way I could levitate or reach out a hand to fetch objects that were far away —but that didn't mean I wanted to discuss them in front of the cold-faced Margaret. She must have been a very good agent or she wouldn't have been working for Max, but I had a feeling she wouldn't have much patience with talk about ghosts and psychic abilities.

"Oh, Calum needed a local guide," I said easily. "He's writing a book."

Those words seemed to make Margaret relax slightly...or at least, she didn't look quite so hostile as she had a moment earlier. "A book?" she said. "What about?"

"Haunted sites across the Southwest," he answered promptly, and at once her expression shut down again.

To my infinite relief, the server showed up then with Calum's and my dinner, and Max quickly excused himself and Margaret so the waitress would have room to approach the table and set down our food. As they left, though, Max sent me another one of those glances over his shoulder, the kind of look that told me he would definitely be chatting me up on the topic of Calum McRae sooner rather than later.

After we'd settled ourselves back at the table, Calum said, "You didn't mention you were friends with Max Sullivan."

Maybe I shrugged slightly. "We grew up next door to each other. He came back to Las Vegas last fall to shoot a movie and decided to buy a house there."

"Oh, right—that movie where the director was murdered," Calum replied. "I remember that being all over the news for a while."

Yes, it had. But with Max exonerated and Evan Bryant safely in prison, the paparazzi who'd haunted my friend during those first few weeks after he came back to New Mexico had now mostly departed. Every once in a while someone would try to shadow him, trying to get lord knows what kind of story, but because he'd have either Al or Lou shut them down, that would be the end of it...until the latest ambitious photographer tried to take a stab at their elusive prey.

What they were trying to find, I didn't know, because Max lived a pretty quiet life in Las Vegas. He had his horses and his garden to work on during the warm months, and all the locals were so used to his presence by now that the only people who batted an eye when they encountered him were the tourists.

"But you've stayed friends?" Calum inquired.

Was there some angle to this line of questioning that I hadn't quite figured out? Nothing in his expression indicated anything except simple interest, but I couldn't quite understand why he should care whether or not Max Sullivan and I were friends.

Unless...was he jealous?

No, that was an absolutely ridiculous thought. True, Calum seemed as if he must be at least partly interested in me, or I doubted he would have asked me out to dinner two nights in a row, but....

"Sure," I said easily. "Or I suppose it's more like we renewed our friendship after he came back to Las Vegas. We didn't really talk when he first left for Hollywood, but he was super busy."

"Becoming a movie star," Calum remarked

with a curl of his lip. He reached for his sangria and took a swallow, then picked up one of his tacos.

"Basically, yes," I said. It seemed like a good time to change the subject, so, after I'd reached for my fork, I added, "Are you going to keep focusing on the basement, or are you going to take readings in other parts of the hotel?"

Calum's mouth quirked again—he'd clearly seen my obvious change of subject for what it was —but to my relief, he didn't call me out for abruptly dropping the topic of Max Sullivan. "I've already been going about with the EMF reader and the voice recorder. So far, I haven't encountered any EVPs in any other parts of the hotel, but the reader definitely spikes up on the third floor, and in another spot on the second floor, outside the John Carpenter room."

Appropriate, I thought, but I didn't comment, only waited for him to go on.

"So it seems as if there's spirit activity on all floors, even if it's not always as spectacular as the laughter that one woman heard or the obvious presences we sensed down in the basement." He paused there to take a bite of taco, then went on, "I'm fairly certain that's Byron T. on the third floor, but I'll have to do more research to see who might be hanging out on the second level...and to find out who 'A.M.' was."

"What if you can't?" I asked frankly, and

Calum rewarded me with another of his cheerfully lopsided grins.

"I might not," he said, and didn't seem too dismayed by that prospect. "That's just part of doing these kinds of investigations. Sometimes you find gold, and sometimes you're left with more questions than you had when you started."

It seemed like a kind of frustrating field of work, but since even my short acquaintance with Calum had told me he was the sort of person who rolled with the punches, he probably could handle it better than most.

Also, even though he hadn't come right out and said so, I got the impression he was doing this mostly for fun and not because he needed the money.

The rest of our meal was mellow enough, though, and I had to admit I enjoyed the atmosphere, enjoyed being up on the rooftop with those warm summer breezes blowing around us and the lively sound of people's conversations on all sides competing with the reggae-toned music flowing from the cantina's speakers. By the time we were done eating, I'd almost forgotten that little run-in with Max and his agent.

If I could even call it that. Sure, the encounter had seemed kind of tense, but I supposed I could blame that on Margaret. She definitely didn't seem like a party-hearty kind of person, and it felt a little strange for her to have met Max at a place like the Coyote Cantina.

Then again, the venue had probably been his suggestion.

At that time of year, twilight lingered for a long time, so it wasn't even dark yet when Calum and I got into his Land Rover and headed back to Las Vegas. On the way, he talked about other places he planned to visit—the Driskill Hotel in Austin, Texas, and the Stanley in Colorado, the setting for the original *Shining* movie—and I found myself growing a little wistful.

What would it be like to roam the country wherever you liked, and not be tied down to a particular place or job?

As soon as that thought went through my head, I wanted to laugh at myself. I was the original homebody, happy to putter in my house and kitchen, glad to be in a place where I knew almost everyone and they all knew me. I'd never been the kind of person who wanted to put herself out in front, which I'd kind of have to do if I was going to a new place and meeting new people every couple of days.

But the rest of the drive was almost soothing, with the darkening landscape passing by and Calum's soft Scottish burr in my ears. When we parked in front of the Plaza Hotel, he turned off the engine and looked over at me.

"Fancy another drink?"

For a second, I hesitated. No, it wasn't that late —barely nine o'clock—but I knew I should probably tell him goodnight and go home, even though we'd only had one glass of sangria each back in Santa Fe.

On the other hand, I was getting tired of having to be the sensible, responsible one.

"Sure," I said, and he grinned.

"Super. Let's go on in."

I climbed out of the passenger seat and followed him into the hotel, telling myself it wasn't going to kill me if I lost a half hour's sleep or so. Besides, we would have had to come back to this part of town anyway, since my car was still parked in its space behind Levitation Latte.

However, we'd barely entered the lobby before we practically tripped over a scatter of luggage and crates blocking most of the space by the front desk. Presiding over the motley collection was a man who looked like he could have been in his late thirties or early forties, with thinning pale hair and equally pale eyes hidden behind a pair of wire-framed glasses.

"Mason Fowles," Calum said. "What a surprise."

His tone was frosty in the extreme, so unlike him that I sent him a startled glance. The stranger —Mason Fowles, I presumed—glared back at

Calum for a moment, then transferred his scornful gaze to me.

"Consorting with the locals, I see," he said.

Well, I *was* a local, but that didn't mean I liked being referred to so dismissively. I put my hands on my hips, but Calum spoke before I could think of a suitable retort.

"You're not going to find anything here," he said. "So you might as well pack it up and move on."

And he took me by the hand and led me into the bar. Behind me, I caught a glimpse of Mason Fowles glaring in our direction right before a bellboy showed up with a rolling cart to start loading the man's numerous pieces of luggage.

"What was all that about?" I asked after Calum and I were safely seated at a table near the window. At that hour on a weekday night, the bar was nearly deserted, so I didn't have to worry about anyone overhearing us.

Also, I didn't see any sign of Leila, which in a way was reassuring. Her last interactions with Calum had been a little tense, so it just seemed better to not have to deal with her tonight.

Instead, Abby came over and took our orders, and once she was gone, Calum finally answered my question.

"Mason Fowles is another paranormal researcher," he explained. "He thinks he's the shit because he has a degree in parapsychology from the University of Arizona, and he hates amateurs like me 'meddling,' as he puts it."

Well, that explained the man's bad attitude. "It's not like he owns this stuff just because he has a degree," I remarked.

"Yeah, I've mentioned that to him on occasion. It doesn't do much to improve his mood."

No, probably not. "So...why is he here now?"

Calum grimaced, but waited until after Abby had dropped off our drinks—malbec for me and brown ale for my companion—to answer my question. "Because, even though he thinks he's the top dog, he doesn't have an original idea in his head. He's always tagging along after me, trying to horn in on my investigations."

"How does he even know where you're going to be?"

Now Calum's sour expression turned almost cheerful. "Oh, I suppose that's mostly my fault. I like to post bits on my YouTube channel to let people know where I'm going. It's not a state secret or anything. At the same time, though, it's definitely annoying to have Fowles lurking somewhere every time I turn around."

"Is he writing a book, too?" I asked. Bad enough to have the guy following Calum everywhere he went, but if he was copying him by writing his own book, the obvious imitation would only make an irritating situation that much worse.

That question earned me a grin. "Oh, Mason always says he's writing a book, but I've yet to see him actually publish anything. I think it's more of a ploy to pay for his travels than anything else."

Since I knew a couple of people in Las Vegas who also claimed to be writers but who never managed to produce a completed manuscript, let alone have one published, this sort of behavior didn't surprise me too much. "What does he do for a living, then? Is he a professor or something?"

Calum's eyes crinkled with amusement, and he lifted his glass of ale and took a sip. "No. He has a bachelor's, but not a master's, let alone a Ph.D. I think he does something with computers, but as a consultant, not in a regular office job."

Which I supposed would pay enough for him to wander around the Southwest trailing after Calum, and also allow him the freedom to not be stuck at a desk all day. Still, it sounded like the guy really needed to find a different hobby.

"I hope he won't get in your way too much," I said after sipping from my own drink.

"He's more of a nuisance than anything else. Besides, while I talk about my travels on my YouTube channel, I don't actually post any of my research until it's done. There's no way Mason

Fowles will be able to find out what I've been investigating."

Well, unless he decided to pick Leila's brain or something, but I guessed that possibility was pretty unlikely. If she'd wanted Mason on the case, she would have reached out to him. And since Calum was a hundred times friendlier and about a thousand times cuter, it didn't take a rocket scientist to figure out which paranormal researcher she would've contacted first. However, even though she'd pointed him in my direction when he was looking for a local psychic to work with, it sounded as though he'd come to Las Vegas on his own volition, not at anyone's particular invitation.

But I noticed how Calum kept our conversation light and well away from any of the phenomena we'd observed over the past couple of days, as though he was worried that Mason Fowler might be lurking at the entrance to the bar and doing his best to eavesdrop on our conversation.

There was no sign of him as we left, however. Calum insisted on walking me to my car, even though I'd assured him it was perfectly safe, and I had to admit I didn't mind too much.

It was quiet and dark behind the shop, and a perfect spot for a goodnight kiss...if that was even where his intentions lay. So far, I was having a hard time getting a read on him.

When we paused by my Subaru, what I could

see of his expression in the light from the security fixture mounted above the back door was diffident.

"I want to kiss you," he said, and I blinked up at him, not sure how to respond. But before I could say anything, he went on, "It's just that I need to know there's nothing going on between you and Max Sullivan. I don't want to get in the middle of that."

"There's nothing going on," I assured him. "Max and I are just friends."

Calum didn't appear particularly convinced. "That's not the impression I got."

I blinked again. "From me?"

"No," Calum replied. "From Max. I saw the way he was looking at you."

I didn't think he'd been looking at me in any particular way, but then, maybe I was simply too familiar with Max to realize there might be something going on I hadn't noticed.

A thrill of hope went through me at that prospect, one I knew I needed to quash immediately. It was ridiculous to think he might be attracted to me. The two of us were friends, nothing more, and Calum had probably just felt intimidated because I was good friends with someone who was so rich and famous.

The problem with that particular theory was that I doubted Calum McRae had ever been intimidated by anyone in his life.

"Really, we're just friends," I said. "That's it."

For a moment, Calum was silent. Then he bent and kissed me...but only on the cheek, a gentle brush of his lips against my skin.

Even so, that soft touch should have been enough to send a thrill through me. Wasn't I totally attracted to the guy? Hadn't I been thinking only the day before how easy it was to get along with him?

Yes, I had thought that, but apparently my body hadn't gotten the memo.

"Right," he said quietly. "I think I'll leave it there for now. Sleep well, Skye."

And he turned and headed back toward the hotel, while I stood there next to my car and wondered what the hell was wrong with me.

CHAPTER 6

Cold Case

What was wrong with me was that I couldn't take my feelings about Max and hide them in a box. It had been different when he was away in Los Angeles, because I could tell myself he was never coming back and I needed to go on with my life. That was why I'd managed to date a few people, and even had a relationship with Kyle Isaacs, one of the local deputies, that lasted almost six months.

Now, though....

Now, Max was back living in Las Vegas. Sure, he had to leave from time to time to shoot a movie or go on a press junket or whatever, but he'd pretty much told me point-blank that he was done with Southern California's rat race and wanted to make a permanent home for himself here. And with him here, that meant any hope of me being able to have a love life was pretty much dashed. After all, if I couldn't get myself together enough to respond to a kiss from someone like Calum McRae, how much luck would I have with a regular guy from my hometown?

"You're an idiot," I told my reflection in the bathroom mirror, a reflection that didn't appear particularly flushed and happy.

No, I looked more tired than anything else.

Feeling cranky, I climbed into bed but didn't pull up the quilt, only the sheet and the lightweight cotton blanket I used in the summer. In the background, the central air conditioning hummed quietly, although I wasn't sure it would help lull me to sleep tonight.

I really, really wished Deanne was here. She was the only person in the world who understood how I felt about Max, and I knew I could have poured out my troubles to her and gotten some kind of comforting reply.

Unfortunately, this wasn't the kind of discussion I wanted to have via text or even over the phone. Besides, I shouldn't be interrupting her Hawaiian vacation with my angst. She'd earned that time off, and I needed to pull up my big girl panties and get through this thing on my own.

Whatever this thing truly was.

Or maybe it wasn't that I couldn't be with anyone other than Max Sullivan, but more that both my brain and my heart were telling me there wasn't much point in getting involved with Calum McRae, not when it was clear that he didn't have any plans to stay in one place but preferred to roam around the country and conduct his investigations wherever his research led him. Those few stray thoughts in the car ride home aside, I wasn't made for that kind of life. I needed to be someplace safe, someplace familiar.

And that meant Las Vegas.

I huffed out a sigh and rolled over on my side, hoping I might be able to fall asleep better in that position. It must have worked, because not too long afterward, I dreamed.

The dream had the soft sepia tone of an old movie, making me think I was seeing something from a long time ago, even though all I was looking at was the façade of the Plaza Hotel, not much changed from how it appeared now, although the cars parked out front looked like something from a movie set, old Model Ts and other vehicles I didn't recognize.

People walked up and down the sidewalk, men in stiff, old-fashioned black suits, and women in light-colored drop-waist dresses and cloche hats, looking like something out of *Bonnie and Clyde*.

Definitely sometime in the 1920s, although I wasn't a big enough expert on vintage fashion to pinpoint exactly which year it was.

A man was walking up the front steps, a boy and girl in tow. Since his back was to me, I couldn't see the man's face. The children seemed young, maybe seven and five, maybe a little younger. Since they were also facing away, I couldn't really catch a glimpse of what they looked like, although they were both dark-haired, the little girl with long black corkscrew curls that showed up clearly against her white dress.

It looked as though the little girl was tugging at the man's hand, as if she didn't want to go inside. However, he tightened his grip and dragged her along with him, while the boy walked stolidly at the man's side.

Then they went through the door to the hotel. It closed behind them, and at the same time, the dream evaporated.

I blinked, opening my eyes to the familiar sights in my bedroom—the semi-sheer drapes at the window and the faint glow of the streetlights beyond, the soft illumination from the digital alarm clock on my nightstand, its display dimmed for the evening so it wouldn't keep me awake.

Who were those people? Were they the ghosts that inhabited the basement, the little boy and little girl and the older man who accompanied them?

I had to believe so; the man's hair had been as dark as the children's, slicked back with pomade in the style of their times. Because I couldn't see his face, I didn't have any way of knowing exactly how old he was.

But it felt like a true dream because of its sharp details, the way it seemed as though I was looking at a movie rather than the blurry impression of my regular dreams.

What had it been trying to show me? That the stories were true, that there really had been a man and two children who'd perished in the basement, possibly during the boiler explosion?

If that was the case, you'd think at least the darn thing would have revealed their faces.

Even as that grumpy thought went through my mind, I knew it didn't always work that way. The dreams provided hints, images, suggestions. It wasn't like they were a blueprint.

Or a treasure map, with "X" marking the spot.

For a moment, I lay there and stared up at the ceiling, and wondered if I should go downstairs and brew some tea, try to do a reading. Maybe the leaves would reveal what the dream had kept obscured.

But it was past midnight, and I had to get up in a little more than four hours. I didn't want to wander around the house and make tea. No, I just wanted to get some more damn sleep, thank you very much.

So I rolled over again, closed my eyes, and

hoped the rest of my night would be uninterrupted.

Which it was; I awoke to the alarm going off, and that hardly ever happened. Yes, I had to get up at o'dark thirty, but after years of following the same schedule, I was generally able to wake up on my own.

Feeling bleary, I climbed out of bed, took a shower, and went through the rest of the rituals I used to start my morning. I wasn't looking forward to another day of working alone, especially with the images from my dream of the night before crowding in my head. Why had the little girl been tugging at the man's hand, as though she desperately wanted to get away? Had she somehow known the boiler was going to blow?

That theory seemed a little far-fetched, even for me. It was probably something a lot more prosaic, like he'd been taking her to work with him because he didn't have any childcare options. Frankly, I couldn't think of anything more boring than having to sit in that basement while the man shoveled coal into the boiler, or however those things worked.

Because of course back then, the place hadn't

been haunted, so boredom should have been the only thing she'd have to worry about.

I pushed back a shiver and headed in to work, glad that I only had today and tomorrow to get through, and then it would be the weekend.

The weekend when I'd promised to go over to Max's house on Saturday night.

Normally, that wouldn't have been a problem. Now, though, I could only wonder how long Calum planned to stay in Las Vegas. He hadn't really said how many days he intended to be here, and maybe he didn't know.

What if he wanted to go out on Saturday? I could only imagine his reaction if I told him I already had plans to be at Max's house that night. And sure, I was under no obligation to tell Calum anything, but I really didn't like the idea of lying to him, either.

I told myself I was borrowing trouble. If Calum was still around, I'd just let him know I'd accepted Max's invitation before he'd even showed up in town. There was absolutely nothing strange about going over to a friend's house for a barbecue.

Well, except for the part where I had a mad crush on said "friend."

Tilly was still asleep when I showed up at the shop at a little past five-thirty. She opened one cranky green eye and said, "Have you ever thought about opening later in the day? Some of us need our beauty sleep."

Since I'd been listening to the cat complain about my early hours for months now, I only gave a blithe shrug as I started setting out the ingredients for that morning's batch of muffins. The maple bacon ones of the winter had given way to lemon poppyseed and raspberry macadamia nut, although I also made batches of the perennial favorites blueberry and cranberry. I'd also started experimenting with actual desserts, offering eclairs one day and cupcakes the other. They were such a hit that the small batches I made invariably disappeared before noon, so I'd already decided to continue to offer them for the foreseeable future.

A quick look at my phone that morning told me I hadn't missed any texts from Max or Calum... not that I'd really expected to hear from either one of them late last night or early this morning. To be honest, I didn't know whether Max planned to say anything at all about the way he'd bumped into Calum and me in Santa Fe the night before. He might have given me a couple of significant glances at the time, but he also might have decided it was better to let the whole thing go.

Tilly got up and lapped water from her bowl, then shot me some side-eye. "You planning on feeding me any time soon?"

"After I get this batter going," I replied serenely.

"Or you could always go out and scrounge from a few dumpsters."

"I dumpster-dive for lunch," she returned, sounding crankier than ever. "You would know that if you paid any attention."

Reflecting that someone had gotten up on the wrong side of the cat bed this morning, I set down the sifter I was holding and went over to the shelf where I kept Tilly's bag of Science Diet. I poured the recommended quarter cup in her bowl, then returned to my worktable.

"There," I said. "Now you can go forth and conquer the world."

Without replying, the cat went over to her bowl, promptly scarfed down the kibble I'd provided a moment earlier, and then went out through her cat door, letting it close with an audible bang as she left.

I permitted myself an eye roll, since there wasn't anyone around to see it. Every now and then, I had to wonder whether I'd done the right thing by allowing her to keep her powers of speech rather than returning her to the mute animal she'd been back before I started tinkering with my magic.

But I didn't have a lot of time for idle pondering, however, because with Deanne gone, I had to run out and start that morning's first batch of coffee once the muffins were in the oven, and then go around the shop and make sure everything was in order. I'd left it tidy enough the day before, but I wanted to reassure myself there wasn't anything I'd overlooked.

This Thursday definitely promised to be busier than the two days that had preceded it, because I had a steady stream of customers from the time I opened the doors at seven to a little after nine-thirty, when things started to slow down a bit. Just as I was catching my breath, though, Kyle Isaacs walked in.

He was wearing his uniform, so I knew he was on duty. I hadn't seen him the past couple of days, though, telling me he probably hadn't been working. Usually, he was always able to manufacture a reason to swing by and get a cup of coffee and a muffin.

I poured some French roast for him and set a raspberry macadamia nut muffin on a plate, since I knew he had a particular weakness for those.

"I heard you've been hanging out with a ghost hunter," Kyle remarked. He had sandy-brown hair and hazel eyes, and when he was in uniform, he seemed almost way too beige, although I had to admit to myself he was decent-looking enough, if not exactly in Max's league.

Then again, who was?

His comment served to remind me that the Las Vegas grapevine was still going gangbusters. I wondered who'd been talking to him. Leila? Abby?

I'd always gotten the feeling that Leila had sort of a crush on Kyle, even if she never would have admitted to my face that she had a thing for my ex-boyfriend.

"Paranormal investigator," I said, knowing I sounded a little too prim. "But yes, Calum is here investigating the ghosts at the Plaza."

Kyle made a sort of humphing sound before he picked up his cup of coffee and took a sip. "You really believe in that stuff?"

Well, Kyle always had been a nuts-and-bolts kind of guy. That was part of the reason why we'd broken up—I had a hard time getting along with someone who didn't have at least a little dash of whimsy in him.

Oh, and let's not forget our utter lack of chemistry.

"Sure I do," I said easily. "And so do a lot of other people, including most of the people who work at the hotel. They've seen plenty of crazy stuff over the years."

"Have *you?*" Kyle returned. His tone bordered on challenging, but I told myself it was probably because he hadn't had enough caffeine yet.

"Seen things?" I replied, then went on before he could reply, "No, but I've felt stuff. Cold spots. Weird places in the basement. There's definitely something going on in there, even if I can't say exactly what it is."

He didn't respond right away, and I guessed he'd realized that quarreling with me over something so silly wasn't a very good look. After breaking off a piece of muffin and washing it down with more coffee, he said, "Do you think the ghosts have anything to do with the elevator problems they've been having?"

On that particular subject, I wasn't sure what to think. I shrugged, and reached for the iced tea I'd poured myself a few minutes earlier, right before Kyle showed up. "I don't know," I said. "That sounds more like plain old mechanical problems. But it's still scary when it happens."

He nodded solemnly. "Yeah, that sounded pretty bad. Leila told me about what happened to you two."

Well, now I had confirmation that Leila was the one who'd been talking to him, which didn't surprise me too much. She'd always been super-chatty, and having a harrowing story like that to relate while she was gossiping made it so much better. Not that I really cared if she'd been telling all her tales to Kyle. Honestly, I'd be more than happy to have the two of them hook up so he would abandon his utterly hopeless dream of getting back together with me.

I couldn't say anything like that out loud, of course. "I'm just glad we only dropped one floor.

Almost gave me a heart attack, but it wasn't a big enough fall for either one of us to get hurt."

"Thank God for that."

We were in agreement on one thing, at least. I was about to make some kind of reply when my phone pinged from inside my apron pocket.

I sent an apologetic glance at Kyle, and he sort of nodded, as if to give me permission to check my phone.

The message was from Calum.

I think I'm on the trail of something, but I don't want to say what it is until I have more info. Will probably be busy most of the day. Can you meet me at my room around 7?

That was a little later than I usually ate during the week, but I didn't mind. At least tomorrow was Friday, and if I ended up being out later than I normally would on a weeknight, I still only had one workday to get through.

Sure. See you at 7.

Questions were already crowding into my brain, but because Calum had come right out and said he didn't want to talk about it until he had more information, there didn't seem much point in asking him to elaborate.

He sent me a thumbs-up emoji, and I returned my phone to my pocket.

"The ghost hunter?" Kyle asked. He didn't sound as grumpy as he had a few minutes earlier, probably because he'd consumed half his cup of coffee and almost all of the muffin.

"That was Calum, yes," I said. "I guess he's working on something big."

"Big how?"

"I don't know," I said. "He told me we could talk about it later."

It had been on the tip of my tongue to say Calum and I would talk when we saw each other tonight, but I didn't see the point in giving Kyle that much information. He didn't need to know what I was doing in my private life, especially when I knew those particular details would only make him cranky all over again.

He still looked a little irritated, but he'd probably figured out he really wasn't in a position to pry. Instead, he ate the last couple of bites of his muffin, downed the rest of his coffee, and then got up from the stool where he'd been sitting.

"Thanks for the coffee," he said. "I should probably get back to work, though."

"No problem," I replied. "You know I'm always good for free refills."

He smiled a little awkwardly, then headed out. A few months earlier, Chief DeVargas had cracked down on her deputies wasting time on long breaks like the one Kyle had just taken in my coffee shop, but it looked as though he'd decided to stop following that particular rule, or maybe the chief had given up after realizing at least half her officers weren't going to comply anyway.

That was the only real break in the day, and things hummed along easily enough until it came time to close up shop at three-thirty. I'd have to go home, of course, because I had hours and hours until I needed to head out to meet Calum at his hotel room.

Exactly what was he investigating today, anyway?

That particular question wasn't going to get answered until seven o'clock, though, so I did my best to push aside my impatience, to change out of my work clothes and into a pretty black ruffled top and a clean pair of jeans, to fix my makeup and switch my flip-flops for a pair of black leather thongs with some interesting studded details.

All that only took me about a half hour, though, and I found myself wondering if I should try to brew some tea leaves now and see whether they might provide some extra illumination regarding the back-in-time dream I'd had the night before.

Also, since I didn't know how late I was going to be up, having a little caffeine in my system would probably be a good thing.

I went into the kitchen, filled the kettle only halfway so it wouldn't take as long to boil, and then got out the pretty antique teacup and saucer I always used for my readings. And because it was summer and my garden was lush with flowers and other green, growing things, I didn't mind standing at the window and waiting to hear the whistle from my teakettle that would let me know the water was ready.

But it sent me the signal soon enough, and I hurried over and turned off the gas so the water would settle a bit while I got out my box of green gunpowder tea. It was what I tended to use for these readings, and because it was green and not black tea, it didn't have as much caffeine as some other varieties.

Once I'd tapped a teaspoon of tea into the cup, I poured the hot water over it and let it steep. Since I'd have to wait a few minutes for the tea to be cool enough to drink, I took the cup and saucer over to the kitchen table and sat down by the window, letting my mind settle so I would be ready to receive whatever messages the leaves might want to send me.

Doing so was harder than I'd thought it would be, mostly because I couldn't quite keep myself from wondering what was so important that Calum hadn't wanted to meet me at three-thirty after I got off work so we could do more exploring around the hotel.

But the clock told me it was now about a quarter after five, which meant I didn't have a huge amount of time to wait. An hour and a half, and then I could head out to meet him.

I blew on the surface of the tea, holding the image in my mind of the man taking those two children by the hand and leading them into the Plaza Hotel.

What are those children trying to tell me?

A sip, and another. I couldn't gulp the tea, had to make each sip slow and methodical, all while holding that same question in my head. Once I'd drunk most of the liquid inside the cup, I turned it over on the saucer so any remnants could drain away, and then set the teacup right-side up, peering within to see what shapes the leaves left behind had made.

Most of them had clumped together in the bottom of the cup, and were such a featureless blob that they weren't of much use.

However....

An odd little line of leaves marched their away around the inside of the teacup, looking for all the world like a chain someone had dropped inside there.

Hmm.

A chain had several meanings, the most common being unity, signifying possibly a wedding or an engagement, which didn't seem to apply to the scene I'd witnessed in my dream the night before. On the other hand, it could also mean constriction, a sensation of being trapped or held in place.

And I thought of the way the man had gripped the little girl's hand, how it had looked as though he was practically dragging her inside the hotel.

I didn't have the whole picture yet, but it sure seemed to me as though those kids hadn't wanted anything to do with the man.

Who was he?

The dream hadn't shown me any identifying features, anything that would have made the man stand out from the hundreds of other men who'd come and gone from the Plaza Hotel back in the 1920s. Annoying as that was, it was just part of getting signals from dreams. They rarely showed me exactly what I wanted to know, only offered hints and allusions, nothing direct.

I wouldn't call this reading a total loss, though, not when it had confirmed that those children had been with the man under duress, even if I didn't know who they were.

Was one of them the "A.M." who'd scratched their initials in the walls of the hotel's basement? Or had those letters been left behind by one of the workmen who'd built the place, someone who'd wanted to leave his mark on the structure?

Again, impossible to know for sure with the flimsy data I currently had on hand.

But maybe that was what Calum had discovered. I supposed I'd find out soon enough.

Washing the teacup and putting it away only took me a couple of minutes. Since I still had a while before I could leave, I went out to the living room and turned on the TV.

If nothing else, getting lost in a home improvement show sounded like a very good way to forget about everything that was currently happening in Las Vegas.

The street looked crowded as I drove up to the Plaza Hotel—it didn't have a dedicated parking lot —so I circled back and parked my Crosstrek in its usual spot behind Levitation Latte. An odd little breeze, almost but not quite cool, met me as I stepped out of the car, telling me that the monsoon clouds that had been threatening all day were probably about to let loose.

Which was fine. We could use a good rainstorm, and because I usually let my wavy hair go natural unless I had a special event to attend, there wasn't much that getting wet would do to it.

In fact, thunder grumbled overhead as I mounted the steps to the hotel, although I hadn't seen a lightning flash. Most likely, it had hit someplace far away, maybe somewhere way up the mountainside.

Even though the troublesome elevator had apparently been fixed, I took the stairs, figuring it was better to be safe than sorry. It seemed as though I wasn't the only one being careful, because I passed the pinch-faced Mason Fowles as I went up to the third floor. He sent me a baleful glare but didn't say anything, and I couldn't help grinning as I opened the door from the stairwell and made my way out into the corridor.

That guy really needed to switch to decaf.

I headed over to Calum's room and knocked, then waited.

No response.

Frowning, I pulled my phone out of my purse and looked down at the screen. Seven o'clock on the dot, so it wasn't like he could have gotten tired of waiting for me and headed down to dinner by himself.

Maybe he was on the phone and had his earbuds in or something.

I knocked again, saying, "Calum, it's Skye."

Again, no response, not even a stir of movement inside the room that would tell me he was there.

Doing my best to ignore the irritation stirring in me, I got out my phone again and sent a quick text.

Hey, Calum, I'm at your door. Didn't you hear me knock?

The phone's screen showed the message had been delivered, but once again, I might as well have been trying to contact someone on the moon.

Worry began to rear its ugly head. What if he'd tripped and fallen, hit his head on something? I had to admit that scenario didn't seem very likely, especially when you considered that Calum was a healthy guy in the prime of life, but I couldn't think of any other reason why he wouldn't have answered my knocks or my text message.

Trying to fight back my rising anxiety, I hurried down the stairs and went over to the front desk. The man working there was Pedro Montaño, a guy who'd been a couple of years ahead of me in high school and was the hotel's evening manager.

"Hi, Pedro," I said as I approached the desk, and he returned my greeting with a friendly smile. He had a gorgeous head of thick dark hair and warm brown eyes, good-looking in a cheerful kind of way, although his hair appeared kind of mussed at the moment.

Well, maybe he'd had to help some guests wrangle their luggage and hadn't had the time to tidy up afterward.

"Hi, Skye," he replied. "What can I do for you?"

I explained the situation, hoping the whole

time that I didn't sound like some kind of nervous-Nellie girlfriend. Not that I was really Calum's girl-friend, but still.

"Would you mind going up there and checking to see if Calum is okay?" I asked after I'd finished my recitation. "Normally, I would never ask some-thing like this, but—"

"It's fine," Pedro cut in, sounding a little abrupt. Then again, I could see how he might not care whether or not I was being too needy, and just wanted to get this over with so he wouldn't be away from his post for too long. "Let's see what's going on."

He stepped out from behind the desk, and the two of us headed upstairs—via the elevator this time, which made me even more on edge. However, we reached the third floor without inci-dent, and when we got to Calum's room, Pedro pulled one of those electronic key cards out of his jacket pocket.

"This one unlocks all the hotel's doors," he told me as he inserted it in the lock, then removed it once the light flashed green.

The door swung inward, and I followed Pedro inside.

At first, nothing seemed too out of place. Calum's MacBook Air sat closed on the table, and the bed was made and unrumpled.

But then I saw his body lying on the floor, his

green eyes wide open, shocked, face pale and waxy. Even before Pedro uttered, "*Díos mio,*" under his breath and hurried over to Calum's still form, I knew.

Calum McRae was dead...and looked exactly like a man who'd been frightened to death.

CHAPTER 7

Broken Heart

"**J**esus, Skye...I am so sorry," Max said. He put a cup of herbal tea in my hands, carefully wrapping my fingers around it as though he was afraid I might let it drop straight to the floor if he didn't take that particular precaution.

For all I knew, he might have been right. God knows I was feeling rattled enough that I wasn't really sure what I was doing.

I'd stood there while Pedro got out his phone and called 9-1-1, had looked on mutely when the paramedics showed up with a couple of deputies in tow. Neither of the police officers had been Kyle, who was obviously off shift by then.

They'd asked a few questions, but it seemed pretty clear that no one suspected me of any wrongdoing. How could they, when it was obvious

Calum had died in a locked room of what they called an apparent heart attack?

They did seem interested when I mentioned that I'd passed Mason Fowles heading downstairs just as I was going up to meet Calum. True, Mason hadn't seemed as though he was in much of a rush, but if he really was connected to Calum's death somehow, he probably would have tried to act as natural as possible.

I wanted him to be responsible. At least that would make some sense, even if I couldn't quite figure out how he could have managed to make Calum look as though he'd died of natural causes while sitting behind a locked door.

Pedro had stayed with me until they took Calum's body away in an ambulance—to the medical examiner's in Albuquerque, I assumed, because sparsely populated San Miguel County, where Las Vegas was located, wasn't populous enough to have one of its own. When an apparently healthy man in the prime of life dropped dead, obviously, they'd need to perform an autopsy.

Leila, who'd been working in the bar, had come over and hugged me, asked me if there was anything I needed. In a daze, I told her no, that I just wanted to go home.

Which I had, although if anyone had asked me exactly how I'd gotten there, I didn't know whether I would have been able to give them a clear answer. I must have driven, but I couldn't remember anything about the trip, only that I was too shaky to deal with opening the garage door once I got to the house—I still hadn't replaced the old, rickety lift-up door with an automatic one—and so had left my car in the driveway.

I honestly didn't remember calling Max, either, but I must have, because he showed up fifteen minutes later, told me to sit down, and then made me a cup of herbal tea.

"Do you want anything else?" he asked once he was back in the living room and had handed the tea to me. "You said you were supposed to meet Calum for dinner. Are you hungry?"

Food was about the last thing on my mind right then. I shook my head, and Max sat down in one of the armchairs that faced the couch, expression grave.

"You'll need to eat sometime," he said.

"I know," I replied drearily. "But honestly, I think if I tried to eat something right now, I'd throw up."

His mouth tightened a little, but at least he didn't try to argue with me. "Okay. Do you want to talk about it?"

"What's to talk about?" I asked, still in that drab little voice which didn't sound very much like mine. "Calum McRae dropped dead out of nowhere. Kind of crazy when you think about it, I suppose."

"Well, that's one way to put it," Max said. "You said it was a heart attack?"

I sipped some tea. Honestly, it tasted like dishwater, but at least it was warm, soothing as it went down my throat.

What wasn't so soothing was the lightning that flashed overhead, followed by a boom of thunder. I flinched and gripped the cup a little tighter.

"I don't know for sure if it was a heart attack," I said. "I suppose that's something the medical examiner will find out. But...Max, he looked like someone who'd been frightened to death. What else could it have been?"

He rubbed a hand over the knee of his jeans, seeming way too uncertain to be Max Sullivan, action star and worldwide box office phenomenon. "Do you think he saw something? A ghost?"

Judging by the faintly skeptical tone in his voice, I got the feeling Max hadn't been sure whether he should even ask that question. "The place is definitely haunted," I said, emphatically enough to let him know I was standing firm on that particular point. "But Calum was the kind of guy who spent his life researching haunted places. I was ready to run from the hotel's basement, it was so creepy, but he acted like it was a walk in the park."

For a moment, Max was silent, apparently absorbing that piece of information. "Did you actually see anything down there, though?"

"No," I said. "It was mostly creepy-crawly sensations."

"Well," he replied, "maybe Calum wasn't as sensitive to the space as you were. Maybe it wasn't until he was confronted by something he could actually see that he was truly frightened."

I supposed that theory made some sense, but I still wasn't buying it. Not when it seemed to me like Calum had been the kind of guy who could walk into a scene from *The Exorcist* without batting an eye.

But then, it wasn't as if I'd known him really well. For all I knew, he'd exaggerated his other encounters with spirits, and then when he was confronted by the reality of some gruesome specter from beyond the grave, his heart just couldn't take it.

"It's possible," I allowed, knowing I shouldn't continue to argue that Calum was incapable of being scared to death when I didn't have all—or any—of the facts at hand. "But he seemed like he was in such good health. I mean, he spent one of his first days here hiking around up in Storrie Lake State Park. Does that sound like someone with a heart condition?"

"No," Max replied immediately, which relieved

me a little. No matter what else was going on, it seemed pretty clear to me that he wasn't here to argue or prove a point, only to offer me whatever support he could.

I told myself I'd only called him because Deanne was thousands of miles away and he was my closest friend in Las Vegas next to her, but I didn't know whether the situation was really that simple. My unrequited crush on him complicated things, true, but there was still something very solid and reassuring about Max's presence, something that made me think he could face down a whole army of creepy spirits out of the *Conjuring* franchise without even breaking a sweat.

"I'm sure the medical examiner will figure it out," he went on. "But I have a feeling it'll turn out to be something completely unconnected to the Plaza Hotel's ghosts."

Remembering how I'd passed Mason Fowles on the stairwell, the way he'd sent me that baleful stare, I wanted to believe Max as well. It would be easy to think this had everything to do with professional rivalry and nothing at all to do with whatever was haunting the historic hotel.

All my instincts, however, were telling me it wouldn't be that easy.

Max stayed with me until almost ten, and even got me to eat a few pieces of sourdough toast with homemade blackberry jam. He also surprised me by offering to sleep on the couch and keep watch through the night, although I told him that wasn't necessary.

"I'm fine," I told him. "And I'll sleep with my phone on the nightstand. If anything gives me the heebie-jeebies, I'll call you."

"You're sure?" he asked, and I nodded.

"Totally," I replied. "Besides, I still have to get up and go to work in the morning. You don't want me waking you up at four-thirty, do you?"

His look of dismay at that prospect almost made me chuckle.

Almost.

"No, I guess not," he said. "But call me if anything weird happens, okay?"

"Okay."

After that exchange, he left, and I locked the door behind him...and lit every white candle in the house, since I'd read somewhere that white candles were good for protection.

And to be honest, even though it freaked me out a little to be alone after everything that had happened that day, I wasn't sure whether I would have slept any better knowing Max was crashed out on the couch in the living room.

Even an entire floor away, he could be pretty distracting.

To my surprise, though, I actually slept just fine, a slumber uninterrupted by any troubling dreams or visions. In fact, I probably would have remained happily conked out until seven o'clock or later if my alarm clock hadn't woken me up.

That Friday at the coffee shop was probably one of the strangest I'd ever spent at work, though. The Las Vegas gossip grapevine had obviously been working overtime, because I could tell from the subdued, almost timid way people interacted with me that my customers had heard the news but weren't sure how they should act. Yes, a man had died, someone I'd spent some time with over the past couple of days, but it wasn't as though Calum and I were lifelong friends or even casually dating.

To be honest, I wasn't sure I knew exactly what we'd been doing. We'd worked together on a project, yes, and maybe a few sparks had flown, but that was about it. I was shocked and sad, and yet this wasn't like losing a family member or a close friend, and I didn't know exactly how I was supposed to feel.

Judging by the way the coffee shop's patrons were acting that day, I could tell they were just about as befuddled by the situation as I was.

I didn't see Kyle until the afternoon, and I guessed he must be working the late shift that

Friday night. "Iced coffee?" I asked as he came in. It was just before two, and therefore after the midday rush.

He shook his head. "Iced tea, thanks. Any ham and cheese croissants left?"

Those had been gone by twelve-fifteen. "No, sorry," I told him. "How about a regular one, or a banana nut muffin?"

"A muffin, then."

I poured him some iced tea, and, after a moment's hesitation, went ahead and put the muffin on a plate. Kyle didn't seem to be in any particular hurry, so I figured it was safe to act like he planned to be here for at least a little while rather than running right back out to his squad car.

After I'd set the muffin and iced tea in front of him—and secretly wondered whether they were his lunch—he spoke again.

"I guess Mason Fowles was arrested this morning."

That piece of news made my eyes widen. "He was?" I responded. My first thought was that it seemed strange no one had mentioned the man's arrest to me, but then again, it wasn't as if the guy knew anyone else in town, and I guessed the deputies who'd taken him in had done their best to keep his apprehension on the down-low.

Kyle sipped some of his iced tea, and then broke off a piece of muffin. He always ate them that way, rather than lifting the whole pastry to his mouth and taking a bite. "That's what I heard. He's supposed to be arraigned this afternoon. I guess it was your tip about seeing him in the stairwell that convinced Chief DeVargas there was enough evidence to bring him in for questioning. When Jack and Mike showed up to take him to the station, Fowles started yelling at them and fought back when they tried to get him to leave his room. That's why he's in jail right now, for resisting arrest."

Fighting with deputies did seem like something Mr. Fowles would do. I knew next to nothing about the man, but I'd already gotten the impression he was his own worst enemy.

"So, not for murder?" I said. "Because Mason Fowles sure seemed to hate Calum like poison."

Kyle gave me a lopsided smile. "Not yet, anyway," he said. "I mean, I heard he made some choice blog posts about what a hack Calum McRae was and actually threatened him in some ghost-hunting forum—said something about 'putting him out of business permanently'—but I don't know whether the Chief thinks that's a solid enough motive."

Calum hadn't mentioned anything about any online threats, but I could see why he might have wanted to ignore those interactions, and had probably thought they weren't anything more than bluster on Mason's part. However, if Mason Fowles really had come to Las Vegas for the express purpose of murdering his perceived rival, you would have thought he'd delete all those blog posts —and nasty comments—beforehand in order to get rid of any incriminating evidence.

Then again, maybe he had gotten rid of them. The problem was, stuff on the internet was forever...if you knew the right place to look.

"Did Mason say anything about what happened?"

"Doesn't sound like it," Kyle replied. He swallowed another bite of muffin, washing it down with his iced tea. "He keeps saying he's innocent— not that that's any real surprise. I think he's already been assigned a public defender, but that's about all I know."

"Well, it's a lot more than I knew before you came in," I said, and Kyle's expression immediately perked up at even those small words of praise. "And I'm glad you were able to get him behind bars. He seems kind of unstable."

"No kidding," he said. "The guy doesn't seem very smart, because he's just made himself look that much more guilty. But I guess we'll just have to wait and see what happens."

I guess so, I thought, and held back a skeptical head shake.

Because even though he was sure acting like a

guilty man, something wouldn't stop telling me that Mason Fowles wasn't the one who'd killed Calum. I kept those doubts to myself, though. Even Kyle's enduring hope that we might get back together wasn't enough to make him believe in my gut instincts...even if those same instincts had helped me track down the murderers in three previous cases.

"What happens after the arraignment?" I asked.

Kyle shrugged. "The judge will either grant bail, or he won't. I don't know much about this Mason Fowles guy, but since he's from out of state, he still seems like kind of a flight risk. But that's not my decision to make."

Having delivered that observation, Kyle finished off the rest of his muffin and all of his iced tea. He sent the empty glass a wistful glance, prompting me to say, "Want me to get you a go-cup for the road?"

"Thanks, that would be great," he responded at once. "I have my regular cup in the car, but since I had coffee in it last, the tea probably wouldn't taste very good."

"No worries," I told him as I got out a plastic cup and matching lid, and filled the cup with ice and tea. After I tightened down the lid and fetched a straw from under the counter, I handed them both over.

Another thank-you, and then Kyle headed out to his squad car, which I could see was parked one space up from the front of my shop. As the door closed behind him, I found myself frowning.

Why was I so certain Mason Fowles wasn't the killer? He certainly wasn't going to win any congeniality contests any time soon...and lashing out at a couple of cops just trying to do their jobs wasn't helping his case, either.

Maybe that was the point, though.

It didn't look as if I was going to get many customers this late in my workday, so I went ahead and started tidying up—wiping down tables, restocking the napkin holders, and emptying the trash. However, I knew better than to try clearing out the case with its forlorn three or four muffins left behind, because experience had taught me if I did that, I'd inevitably have someone come in and want one just as I started to lock the door at three-thirty.

In fact, right at five minutes before closing, a woman came into the shop. However, one glance at her told me she wasn't here for a last-minute blueberry muffin or iced latte.

She was wearing an impeccable mint-green sleeveless linen dress and delicate nude sandals, and didn't look like the sort of person you'd normally see wandering around downtown Las Vegas, New Mexico. But her hair was a dark, burnished red that I'd only seen on one other person in my entire life, and when she removed her sunglasses, they revealed eyes almost the same shade of green as the dress she wore, although they were reddened, as if she'd been crying recently.

Well, I thought I could understand the reason behind her sad expression.

Since I didn't want to jump to conclusions, however, I only said, "Can I help you?"

The woman managed a very watery smile. "Are you Skye O'Malley?"

I nodded. "Yes, I'm Skye."

She blinked and pulled in a breath, as though to steady herself. "Hi, I'm—I'm Kate McRae, Calum's sister."

"Oh, I'm so sorry," I said quickly, and she gave me another one of those smiles that looked as though it was about to dissolve into tears at any second.

"Thank you," she replied, and paused so she could root around in the oversized Louis Vuitton bag she had slung over one shoulder. After producing a tissue from a travel pack, she used it to dab at her eyes and nose. "The police chief said you were supposed to meet Calum last night."

I'd never spoken to Chief DeVargas directly, but that didn't mean much. I was sure the deputy who'd taken my statement had passed that information along to her. "Yes. I was helping him with his investigation here."

Kate nodded. "That's what she said. Did he —" She stopped herself there, as if trying to find the right words. Although I'd just met the woman —I guessed she must be Calum's older sister, since she looked as though she was probably four or five years older than I was, polished in a way I knew I could never hope to be—I could tell she was doing her best to hold it together in the face of such a horrible loss. "Did he seem sick at all? Over-tired?"

"Not at all," I told her, even as I went over to the front door so I could lock it. The last thing I wanted was someone coming in while Kate McRae and I were having such a private conversation, and besides, it was now three-thirty anyway, and anyone wandering by could get their refreshments at the hotel or one of the other restaurants on Bridge Street. "He was full of energy. I'd only just met him, but he seemed like the kind of person who didn't let anything slow him down."

"Yes, that sounds like Calum," she said, and her mouth even lifted ever so slightly at the corners, as if part of her wanted to smile. "Which is why this whole thing is so crazy. When I got the call last night—" Another pause, another breath to steady herself. "Our parents travel a lot," she added, as though she needed to explain why she was the one who'd come on this grim errand, "and that's why he had me as his emergency contact. I flew out this morning and rented a car in Albuquerque."

In a way, that was some of the worst of it. Bad enough to suffer such a loss, and so much harder to have to keep it together in order to make travel arrangements and head out of state and do all the other million little things that needed to happen when someone died unexpectedly.

"Anyway," she continued, "I didn't want to believe it was real. It wasn't until I had to...had to talk to the medical examiner that it really hit home."

I realized then that we were still standing a few feet away from the door, and there were more comfortable places to be having this conversation. "Would you like to sit down?" I asked. "I can get you a coffee or an iced tea...anything you like."

Kate gave me another of those wan smiles. "An iced tea would be good. Thank you."

"It's no problem."

And it really wasn't, since I hadn't yet dumped out the pitcher of iced tea or cleared the ice machine to get it ready for the weekend. While Kate went and sat down on one of the purple couches in the far corner of the shop, I hurried behind the counter and poured an iced tea for her, and another for myself.

With both of them in hand, I walked over and

sat down on the couch opposite where she'd seated herself, then extended one of the glasses to her.

"Thank you," she said again, as if it was easier for her to keep repeating those empty words of courtesy than have to return to an obviously painful discussion.

Maybe I could have danced around the issue, but since she'd brought it up....

"Does the—" I paused there, sipped some tea, and then made myself go on, "does the medical examiner have a cause of death yet?"

With a shaky hand, Kate lifted her own glass and drank some of her iced tea. "Yes. We don't have the formal report, but because there was an obvious physical cause, it's not like we have to wait for toxicological tests or anything like that."

"'A physical cause'?" I repeated.

She nodded, eyes a little too bright. Without answering me, she set down her tea on the coffee table in front of us, got out another tissue, and dabbed away the tears that had begun to form once again.

"I guess he had a congenital heart valve defect," she said. "It wasn't detected when he was born, and since he always seemed healthy and happy, our parents never had any reason to have his heart checked. The medical examiner says he can't know for sure exactly what happened, but most likely, the flow of blood to Calum's heart was slowly getting cut off, and all it would have taken was a single shock for him to have a heart attack."

A single shock....

No wonder Calum looked like a man who'd been frightened to death. As far as I could tell, that must have literally been what had happened.

"I'm so sorry," I murmured again, and Kate drew in a breath.

"It's...it's hard. But at least he was here, doing something he loved." Her gaze moved away from me. "What were you investigating, exactly?"

"The ghosts at the Plaza Hotel," I said, and inclined my head toward the wall behind her, even though we obviously couldn't see the hotel from where we sat. "We hadn't gotten very far, though."

"Was it a ghost?" she asked. "That is, whatever startled him."

"I don't know for sure," I replied. "I mean, I've had some creepy experiences in that hotel, but I've never actually *seen* anything. And Calum was with me down in the basement where it was really scary, but he didn't seem too worried about the whole thing. That's why I'm having a hard time trying to wrap my brain around him being literally scared to death."

It was only after the words escaped my lips that I realized how awful they must have sounded. I started to stammer an apology, but Kate only shook her head.

"It's all right," she said, again with that small quirk in the corner of her mouth. "Or, I guess it isn't all right, but since it sounds as though that's what happened, I can't really get mad at you for putting it that way."

She was being way too gracious, considering how I'd just stuck my foot firmly in my mouth.

"Anyway," she went on, "I'm only here to handle the arrangements. Calum wanted to be cremated, but I'm still having him flown to L.A. so our parents can see him one last time. They're already on their way back from Bali."

I nodded, not sure what else I could say, or what Kate even wanted from me. Maybe all she'd needed was to talk to someone who'd been around her brother in those last couple of days before his death.

The real reason for her visit was revealed in the next moment, however, as she reached into her big Louis Vuitton bag and pulled out a MacBook Air not too dissimilar from the one sitting on the desk in my office at home, although it looked like Calum had opted for the slightly bigger screen.

"Chief DeVargas released this to me, along with the rest of Calum's effects," Kate explained as she set it down on the coffee table. "I'm not a ghost hunter, so I doubt I could make sense of whatever he had on here. But I was thinking maybe you could try taking a look."

I stared back at her, not sure what she was asking. "Do you have the password?"

"No. But Calum wasn't super careful about that kind of thing, so it shouldn't be too hard to get into it."

"I'm not a computer hacker," I protested.

Now Kate smiled for real. "I'm not saying you are. You know more about this ghost stuff than I do, though, and that means you'll probably have a better idea of what he could have used for a password."

I wanted to say that simply because Calum was into ghosts and I had a passing interest in the supernatural, it didn't mean I could snap my fingers and come up with his password, just like that.

But her reddened green eyes—so like her brother's—were imploring me to do that very thing, and I thought I understood. She wanted someone else to take this burden from her so she wouldn't have to carry it alone.

"I'll do what I can," I said softly. "Are you staying here in town?"

"At the Castañeda," she replied at once, obviously relieved that I wasn't going offer any further arguments. "I couldn't stay at the hotel where he... where he...."

"I totally understand," I assured her.

"But I'm leaving tomorrow morning with

Calum," Kate went on, her tone now brisker as we discussed logistics. "It sounds as if your police have arrested that jerk Mason Fowles for being involved somehow, but I don't need to stay here while they're getting that figured out. I just want to take Calum home." She paused, and added, "You can reach me at 310-555-7788."

I quickly scooped my phone out of my apron pocket and entered her information. It was strange to see her name sitting right below Calum's in my contact screen, and I hurriedly set the phone down on the coffee table next to the MacBook Kate had placed there a few minutes earlier.

It seemed that now she had taken care of that piece of business, she was ready to move on. She stood, brushing at a couple of wrinkles her green linen dress had picked up while we were sitting, and said, "Call me if you find something."

I promised her I would, then went over to the door so I could unlock it and let her out. Once I'd relocked it and pulled down the shades on the front window, my gaze returned to the MacBook Air, innocently sitting on the coffee table.

What are you hiding? I thought.

Only time would tell if I'd ever learn the answer to that question.

CHAPTER 8

Up in the Air

After scooting Tilly into the passenger seat of my Crosstrek—she generally went home with me on the weekend whether she liked it or not —I drove to my house, thoughts roiling. Unlike Kate McRae's fancy bag, my purse wasn't big enough to hold Calum's MacBook Air, so I'd set it on the back seat and admonished Tilly not to walk on it.

"Like I would," she said scornfully. "Why would I want to step on something hard and flat like that?"

Good question. However, considering her tendency to roam wherever she wanted, I'd thought it safer to tell her the laptop was hands—or paws—off.

When we got home, the cat jumped out of the car, promptly scurried across the driveway, and ran to Max's parents' house next door, where she disappeared over the fence. Since that was her normal behavior whenever I brought her home—well, as long as the weather was nice—I wasn't too worried about her defection. She'd come back and let herself in via the cat door as soon as she decided it was time for dinner.

As for myself, I didn't know quite what to do. Max had texted me during the day, checking to see if I was all right, wanting to know if I was still coming to his place to barbecue the following night, or whether we should move our dinner up to today if I didn't want to be by myself. I'd told him I was fine and planned to have a quiet evening in, but that I'd see him Saturday at six.

At the time, I'd thought I was being very grown-up and mature, and proving that I was doing okay by not changing our dinner plans. Now, though, as I stood there in my empty house, I wanted to kick myself for being such an idiot.

My pride wouldn't let me call Max, though, so I went into the kitchen and got myself a glass of water. I'd set Calum's laptop on the kitchen table next to my purse, which meant I couldn't exactly ignore its presence.

Did Kate really think I was smart enough to hack into the thing?

Not "hack," I told myself. Just figure out what Calum could have used for a password. She herself *said he wasn't careful about that kind of thing, so it's not like I have to figure out some ten-digit automated password or anything like that.*

Put that way, the task didn't seem quite so daunting.

All the same, it was Friday evening after a *very* long week, and I'd earned a little liquid courage.

I set my glass of water on the countertop and then reached into the cupboard to get one of the fun "confetti"-style Mexican stemless glasses I'd bought about a month ago on a whim. There was a partially drunk bottle of chardonnay in the fridge, so I poured an inch or so into the glass, then took it with me over to the kitchen table.

A couple of sips gave me the necessary backbone to open Calum's laptop. However, I didn't see the same bright pink and purple login screen that greeted me when I started up my own laptop, but a desert scene with a moon over it, the arched rock formations telling me it looked like something out of Monument Valley.

What wasn't so pretty was the little login rectangle that blocked part of the screen. His name was filled in, telling me he'd probably been logged in and working on the computer when he suffered his heart attack. What I didn't know was the setting he'd used to require the password to be entered after a certain amount of time had elapsed. Since I lived alone and pretty much never took my laptop out of the house, I had mine set at an hour.

But Calum could have used the same setting, or he could have made it so the MacBook Air required him to re-authenticate every time he closed the lid. Locked out like this, it was impossible for me to tell.

The good thing was, unlike my iPhone, the MacBook didn't have a finite number of login attempts I could use before I bricked the thing, which meant I could go at this indefinitely if I had to.

After all, I had the whole weekend ahead of me, minus my planned barbecue at Max's house on Saturday night.

Even so, I sat there for a long time, staring at the login screen. Although I had his sister's express permission to get into the computer, something about this seemed wrong, invasive. After all, I didn't know much about Calum McRae, when you got right down to it. What if he had some kind of awful internet porn stored on his laptop?

I didn't really want to acknowledge the thought, so I pushed it back to the darkest reaches of my brain whence it came.

Start easy, I told myself.

All right, then.

"Ghost123" didn't get me in, and neither did "Spirit11" or any other combinations of those words with various numbers. "Haunted" and "Possessed" got me the same results, aka bupkis.

Maybe I was going about this wrong. Maybe he'd used a password from one of the places he'd visited, rather than the phenomena he was going to investigate.

Unfortunately, "Tombstone" and "Austin" and any other place I could remember him mentioning yielded similar results. Feeling desperate, I entered "KateM," but that didn't work, either.

Sure, this was going to be a walk in the park.

I closed the laptop's lid, figuring I should save the battery. Doing so made me realize Kate hadn't given me the charger, and I frowned, then told myself it wasn't that big a deal, since it used the same kind of charger that my own MacBook did.

I headed upstairs to retrieve the accessory from my office, then went back down to the kitchen. Luckily, there was a plug in the wall right below the table, so at least I wouldn't have to move the laptop to get it properly charged.

Another swallow of chardonnay, and I went gamely at it for another half hour or so before I decided my brain had had enough that day. The thought passed through my mind that maybe I should call Kate and see if she had any hints she could give me as to what Calum would think was important enough that he'd use it as his password.

However, I shot that idea down almost at once.

She had enough on her plate to deal with right now, and if I called her so soon after taking a crack at the laptop, it would feel like admitting defeat.

Besides, she'd pretty much said I could keep the MacBook for as long as necessary. Although I'd gotten the impression that she loved her brother very much, it felt to me as though she wasn't all that interested in his work, except where it might provide a clue as to what had frightened him so much that the shock had caused his heart to fail.

I closed the lid, swallowed the last of my chardonnay, and told myself it was okay. A whole weekend lay ahead of me, and that meant I had plenty of time.

———

As it turned out, I didn't have as much free time as I thought. A little after eleven on Saturday morning, my cell phone rang. I picked it up from where I'd left it on the kitchen table by Calum's laptop— now fully charged—and frowned down at the screen. The number was local, but it wasn't Max's or Deanne's...not that she would be calling me at that hour when Hawaii was three hours behind New Mexico. Most likely, she wouldn't even be awake yet.

"Hello?" I said.

"Hi, Skye," came a voice I recognized almost at once.

Darcy Montoya, who worked the front desk at the police station.

I found myself frowning even as she went on, "Sorry to bug you on a Saturday morning, but this guy we have locked up here keeps insisting that he needs to talk to you."

"'Guy'?" I repeated blankly...and then comprehension dawned. After all, it wasn't as though the Las Vegas police station's holding cells were exactly overbrimming with prisoners. "You mean Mason Fowles?"

"Yeah, him," Darcy replied, her flat tone telling me pretty much exactly what she thought of the man.

Since I wasn't exactly a member of the Mason Fowles fan club, either, I could relate. "Why does he want to talk to me?"

"He won't say. I mean, I can get why he's so agitated, because the D.A. just tacked on a murder charge in addition to aggravated assault. I—"

"What...what?" I broke in. "When did that happen?"

"I guess the forensics people found his fingerprints on the door to Calum's room, so that plus the way he went off on David and Mike when they came to talk to them gave Chief DeVargas all she needed to ask the district attorney to amend the complaint." Darcy paused there, and added wryly, "I suppose you can guess how much that improved Mr. Fowles' mood. Anyway, since he's allowed a visitor, I figured I'd call you and see if you'd be willing to come over and see what he wants. Right now, I'd do just about anything to get him to shut up."

Considering that Darcy tended to be a fairly patient person—a quality that stood her in good stead in a public-facing position like hers—I guessed Mr. Fowles must really have been plucking her last nerve.

And because I didn't have anything on the docket for today except doing some laundry and taking another crack at Calum's laptop, I knew I had a half hour or so to spare.

Besides, I wanted to hear what Mason had to say.

"Okay," I said. "I can be over there in about fifteen minutes. I need to put some laundry in the dryer before I head out."

"Thank you so much," Darcy replied, gratitude shimmering in every syllable. "I'll tell him you'll be here shortly."

"See you in a bit," I told her, then ended the call.

Tilly was nowhere to be found when I finished up in the laundry room, but I went ahead and put some food in her bowl anyway. It was close enough to lunchtime, and since I didn't know exactly when I was going to be back, I thought I might as well play it safe.

The drive over to the police station didn't take me very long. In fact, because so many people were out at the park that day and shopping in the stores all along Bridge Street, I had to leave my car almost two blocks away, making the walk to the station take almost as much time as the drive itself had.

It was another hot, sunny day, this one without the promise of monsoon clouds on the horizon to possibly cool things off later in the afternoon. Because of the heat, I was all too glad to enter the police station's air-conditioned splendor...although probably not as glad as Darcy was when she spotted me coming in. At once, she smiled, and stepped out from behind the front desk. She was in uniform, but she always managed to glam it up somehow, this time with her near-black hair in an enormous bun on the top of her head and big CZ-studded hoop earrings that I doubted were regulation dangling from her ears.

Well, it was Saturday, and I doubted Chief DeVargas was anywhere around. That was probably a good thing on multiple levels.

"Thank you so much," Darcy said, as though worried that the thank-yous she'd given me over the phone weren't enough to compensate for making me come over here on a weekend. "I really owe you one."

"I'll remind you of that the next time I get a speeding ticket," I joked, and she just grinned back at me.

We both knew that I'd never gotten a traffic ticket in my life.

"He's back here," Darcy went on, immediately leading me toward the rear of the building where the holding cells were located. I knew that already, mostly because I'd gone back there a few months earlier when I went to talk to Elliott Rosenthal about his sister's murder. He'd been so grateful to me for clearing his name that he'd sent me a big fat check as a thank-you, money I'd spent on my new car before banking the rest.

Somehow, I doubted Mason Fowles would be that gracious for any assistance I might be able to provide.

Almost as soon as we got to his cell, Darcy said quickly, "I'll leave you here to talk. Just try not to take more than a half hour, okay?"

I somehow doubted the time limitation would be a problem.

She turned and practically fled down the corridor, while I pulled in a breath and stepped closer to Mason's cell. At our approach, he'd gotten up from the bed and now stood near the bars, his expression an odd mixture of annoyance and anticipation.

A quick glance around told me he was the only person currently locked up back here, and I supposed that was a good thing. It was probably better to do this without an audience.

"Deputy Montoya said you wanted to talk to me."

Mason sniffed, and halfway looked as though he wanted to comment that the "deputy" didn't seem very professional. But then he appeared to remember where he was, and that both of us were doing him a favor we didn't necessarily think he deserved.

"I did," he said. He seemed to be one of those men who didn't grow a beard very fast, because I couldn't see much stubble on his cheeks despite his night in jail. His hair was mussed, though, and he took off his wire-rimmed glasses to wipe them with the tail of his shirt before he put them back on.

A nervous gesture, or did they really have some smudges on the lenses?

Then he glanced around, as though to reassure himself that we really were the only two people back in the holding area. In an urgent tone, he went on, "I need you to help me get out of here."

For a second, I stared back at him. Then I said, wearing a faint smile, "You mean, like bust you out? I'm not very good at jailbreaking."

His mouth twisted. "You know that's not what

I meant. I didn't kill Calum McRae, and I need you to help me prove it."

Well, the guy had some brass *cojones,* that was for sure. Voice level, I said, "But you definitely assaulted those cops."

His mouth tightened. "I was provoked. I'm innocent. I have no doubt the charges will all be dropped once we can prove who the real murderer is."

Maybe, maybe not. If the only thing that had happened between him and those two deputies was a minor scuffle, then I supposed a good attorney could make it all go away, especially if the murder charges were also dismissed.

Rather than comment on that, I remarked, "Why should I help you? Calum and I were friends."

"'Friends'?" Mason repeated. "You hardly knew the man."

Okay, fair enough. It wasn't as though the two of us had been lifelong besties or anything like that. But we'd been friendly, and I'd thought our relationship was progressing. Exactly where, I hadn't known for sure...and never would...but I still felt comfortable enough calling Calum a friend even if we hadn't known each other for very long.

"I looked on him as a friend," I said steadily, and met Mason's irritated, pale blue gaze head on.

He was the one who glanced away first, and I felt a small stab of satisfaction.

"Well, we don't have to argue semantics," he said, his tone testy. "But I've heard about how you were able to exonerate your movie actor friend, so it seems as though you're the best person to help me now."

Exactly where he'd heard that story about Max, I didn't know. From Darcy herself? From someone at the hotel?

I supposed it didn't matter all that much.

"I thought you were assigned a public defender."

"'Public defender'?" Mason repeated, and gave a derisive snort. "That idiot couldn't get me out of a parking ticket, let alone a murder charge. I need someone who has at least a chance of helping me out of this mess."

It was on the tip of my tongue to tell him I was the last person he should be asking for a favor, considering the way he'd acted toward Calum...and me.

But even though I'd never been suspected of murder, I knew what it was like to have people close to me charged with such a horrible thing. For all his prickly exterior—much like the cacti of his native Arizona, I supposed—I could tell Mason Fowles was afraid, that on the surface, the evidence pointed toward him and no one else.

"All right," I said, doing my best not to sigh. "Let's start at the beginning, then. Why did you come to Las Vegas?"

Mason's gaze slid away from mine. "To research the Plaza Hotel, of course."

I lifted an eyebrow. "Seriously? You expect me to believe you decided to come to Las Vegas out of all the haunted hotels and saloons and houses in the Southwest, at exactly the same time Calum was here?"

He jammed his hands in the pockets of his rumpled khakis. "All right," he muttered, then continued in a clearer voice, "Yes, I followed Calum here. I'll admit the man had a good nose for sniffing out an interesting haunting. But his methods were sloppy, and the evidence he gathered would never stand up in a peer-reviewed journal or anything that had actual standards."

"Maybe not," I said, even though I inwardly bristled at the man's disparaging comments. "I never got the impression that was what Calum was even doing. He was just collecting ghost stories for his YouTube channel."

That defense didn't seem to win me any points, because Mason's eyes narrowed, and he practically sneered at me. "If he'd stuck to that ridiculous channel, I wouldn't have cared. But then he decides he's going to write a book? With no formal training, no experience in such a thing? The whole idea was preposterous."

On the surface, maybe that evaluation of the situation was true. After all, Calum himself had told me he'd started out the whole ghost-hunting thing as a hobby, and definitely didn't have the kind of background that Mason Fowles did.

"Who was he hurting by writing a book?" I asked, and honestly wanted to know the answer to my question. "If it turned out to suck, then no one would buy it."

Mason raised an eyebrow, as though he couldn't believe anyone could possibly be that naïve. "People would buy it because he has...*had*...a huge social media following. And then when they realized they'd wasted their money on a poorly researched piece of junk, they'd trash it, and the ghost-hunting community at large. Do you have any idea how hard it is to get anyone to take us seriously in the first place?"

Since I wasn't a professional ghost hunter, I couldn't say for sure.

On the other hand, I knew what it felt like to be on the fringe. Most people in Las Vegas had accepted my tea-leaf reading as just a minor quirk, but I still knew I was different from everyone in town and did my best to act as normal as possible in public. Even though I could safely say I didn't care for Mason Fowles at all, I had to admit he was kind of brave to get out there and let his freak flag fly...so to speak.

"I understand your concerns," I said carefully. "So, you came to Las Vegas to do your own research. Fine—it's not like Calum had an exclusive contract to research ghosts at the Plaza Hotel. But you have to admit it looks kind of sketchy to have you coming down the stairs just moments after he died."

That comment got me a compressed mouth and a very narrow stare. Then Mason said, "It was dinnertime. What's so strange about going downstairs to get a meal at seven o'clock in the evening?"

All right, he had a point there. "Did you tell the police that?"

"Of course I did. Not that it mattered. As far as your police chief—and the local D.A.—are concerned, Calum McRae and I were professional rivals, and I was spotted leaving the scene of the crime...so to speak. They don't need anything more than that to send me to trial."

"And your fingerprints on the handle of his door?"

That question got me a baleful glare. "You're very well-informed, Ms. O'Malley."

I shrugged. "I know people. What about the fingerprints?"

"I went to talk to Calum earlier in the day, but he was out. All right, I may have touched the handle, tried it to see if it was locked. But since it was, I went on my way."

It was fairly obvious from the tense set of Mason's jaw that he didn't much like making that admission. I had no doubt that if the door hadn't been locked, he wouldn't have had any problem with going inside and snooping around in Calum's notes.

When I didn't immediately reply, Mason continued, pale eyes piercing behind the old-fashioned wire-rimmed glasses he wore. "I know that sounds damning, but I didn't kill Calum McRae. He annoyed me, true, but not to the point of murder. The most I can be accused of is trying to scoop him before he had a chance to publish any of his findings."

A petty motivation, true, but I got the feeling Mason was telling me the truth. He would never have confessed to anything that made him look bad if he didn't believe I was the only person who could help him.

"I'm not sure what I can do," I said slowly, then added before he could cut in, "but I'll work on it. Right now I'm just trying to get into Calum's laptop so I can try to find his notes. He told me only a few hours before he died that he'd found something important, although he didn't say what it was. I'm hoping it was connected to the basement and the initials we found there, but—"

So much for trying to keep Mason from interrupting me. "What initials?" he demanded.

"Someone scratched 'A.M.' into the basement wall," I told him. "Probably one of the workmen who laid the brick down there, but we don't know for sure."

His eyes narrowed again, only this time, I guessed it was because he was pondering this latest piece of information. "How big were the letters?"

"Not very big," I replied, even as I thought Calum and I probably should have measured them. Then again, that basement had creeped me out badly enough that I knew I hadn't exactly been thinking straight while I was down there. I paused as I tried to visualize the scratchings on the wall, and added, "Less than an inch high."

"And where were they?"

"Down close to where the wall meets the floor," I said. "Does it matter?"

"It might," Mason said. "When you're conducting an investigation like this, no piece of evidence is too small."

"Well, let's focus on getting you sprung, and then we'll worry about the initials Calum and I found." I stopped there, wondering if there really was anything I could do. "Did the judge at your arraignment give you a chance to post bail?"

Now the man looked almost shamefaced. If I hadn't seen it for myself, I would never have believed Mason Fowles was capable of wearing such an expression.

"He did," he replied, "but it was for half a million dollars. I don't have that kind of money, and I don't know anyone else who does, either."

Neither did I. Oh, sure, I still had some of the hundred thousand dollars Elliott Rosenthal had sent me, but I'd spent a good chunk of it buying my Crosstrek for cash, and the rest was squirreled away in my savings account. While I didn't think Mason was guilty, I also didn't feel like forking over almost all of my money to some bail bondsman.

Then I wanted to smack myself. It was true that the vast majority of my acquaintance didn't have that much money lying around...and it was also true that I knew someone who did, someone who would never miss the fifty thousand dollars we'd need to get Mason Fowles out of jail.

"No worries," I said with a smile. "I know exactly who can pay your bail. In fact, I'm going to see him tonight, so I'll ask him then."

Mason blinked at me, obviously taken aback. "Who?"

"Max Sullivan," I replied.

CHAPTER 9

Fifty Love

Max stared at me in astonishment. "You want me to do *what?*"

"I want you to pay Mason Fowles' bail," I said calmly.

We were sitting outside on one of Max's ranch's patios, the one where we were shaded from the sun by a pergola draped with grapevines overhead. Just as we often did when we sat out here, we were drinking some of his amazing homemade sangria, although he had a bottle of zinfandel set aside for us to have with our steaks.

"Why?" he said.

"Because I know he didn't kill Calum, and he might be able to help me figure out what Calum found before he died."

For a second or two, Max didn't say anything, only gazed back at me from the chair where he sat.

A swallow of sangria, and then he asked, "And you know Mason Fowles is innocent because...?"

"I don't have any concrete evidence one way or another, if that's what you're asking," I replied. "It's just a gut feeling. But you know my gut feelings are pretty accurate."

"Most of the time," Max said. There wasn't any accusation in his tone, though. No, he was simply pointing out the obvious. If I truly batted a thousand all the time when it came to following my intuition, then I would have known early on that Justin Hale was no one to be trusted.

I shrugged, since there wasn't much I could say in response to my friend's comment. All I could do was wait and see whether he was willing to pitch in to get Mason Fowles out of jail.

Because it was Max, he didn't leave me hanging for too long. "Okay," he said. "It's only fifty grand, and you seem convinced this guy might be able to help you."

"Only" fifty grand. I could say with one hundred percent certainty that Max Sullivan was the only person in my circle who could make a comment like that and not mean it ironically.

"I know it's a big ask," I said.

Max shrugged. "I hope you know where to find a bail bondsman around here."

I actually didn't, but that was the sort of thing I could look up on my phone.

Or I could just call Darcy Montoya and ask her for her personal recommendations.

"I'll check into it," I told Max. "But I also told Mason that even if you agreed to help out with his bail, we wouldn't be able to do anything about it until sometime tomorrow." Max's brows lifted slightly, and I hurried to add, "I mean, if you don't have anything else going on."

Now he smiled. "Nope, my schedule is wide open. I was thinking about going riding early before it gets too hot, but that's about it."

Relieved that he seemed just fine with the situation, I picked up my sangria and took a sip. Even though we were protected by the vines that grew across the top of the pergola, the air was still hot and dry, and the cool, fruity drink felt wonderful going down my throat. "If all your Hollywood friends could see you now," I remarked with a grin.

He shook his head. "I'll bet some of them would be secretly envious to have a chance to kick back and relax, instead of going to another premiere or press junket or whatever. But I don't really care what they think."

"You don't?"

Honestly, I didn't even know why I'd asked the question. Max had always been one of those people who sailed serenely through life without worrying about other people's expectations. It wasn't that he didn't care, but more that he wasn't about to let the opinions of others slow him down.

His bright blue eyes glinted at me, and he lifted his own glass of sangria and had a swallow. "Nope. Besides, I'm hardly the first actor to decide he doesn't want anything to do with Hollywood and disappear into the hinterlands. I mean, Harrison Ford's been living in Montana for something like forty years."

Right. I supposed I should have thought of that. And when you got to be a star at Max's level —or Harrison Ford's—it wasn't as though you couldn't have houses spread out all over the world if that was what made you happy.

"One thing, though," Max said, and a little quiver of worry went through me.

Was he going to back out of his offer to cover Mason Fowles' bail?

As soon as that thought popped up, though, I pushed it aside. Once Max gave his word about something, he kept it.

"What?" I asked, doing my best to sound casual.

"Why is all this so important to you?" he asked. "Was there something going on between you and Calum McRae? Is that why you think you need to solve this particular mystery?"

Max's tone was so studiously neutral that a sudden wild hope flared in me.

Was he asking because he really was worried I'd started to fall for Calum?

No, it had to be something else.

"Someone died under mysterious circumstances," I said, and although I really wanted to pick up my glass of sangria and allow myself a healthy swallow, I knew doing so would be an obvious tell that I wasn't quite as casual about the situation as I wanted Max to believe. "That's kind of become my thing."

"And that's all."

Again, his tone was almost too flat. "Well, I *did* know the guy," I remarked. "Not well, but we'd worked together for a couple of days. That gave us something of a connection. But it's not like we were dating or anything."

For a long moment, Max was quiet. His finger ran over the water beaded on the side of his glass and his gaze was intent on the motion, as if the patterns he was drawing in the condensation somehow contained the secrets of the universe.

Then he said, "Good," still not looking at me.

I blinked. "'Good'?" I repeated. "What's that supposed to mean?"

At last, he looked up. The eyes that met mine were so clear and bright, they looked as though they'd been carved from the sapphire-blue expanse overhead. "Because when I saw the two of you in Santa Fe the other night, I realized something."

For some reason, my heart began to beat a bit faster. "You did?"

"Yeah," he said, and flashed a smile at me, the same smile that made women across the world swoony. "I realized I was jealous. I didn't like seeing you with Calum McRae because I wanted to be the one sitting across that table from you."

I stared at him, frozen in place as though I'd been turned to stone, even as my brain started to fire at about thousand miles an hour.

Was this really happening? Had Max Sullivan just admitted he'd envied Calum in that moment, had wanted to trade places with him?

"I...I don't understand," I stammered. Between the heat and the half glass of sangria I'd just drunk, this whole scene was starting to feel unreal, like something I might have experienced in a wistful dream.

But no, this was real, from the rings of water on the granite tabletop to the sound of the wind rustling in the cottonwoods that grew a few yards away.

A tiny drop of perspiration worked its way down the back of my neck, but I didn't reach up to blot it.

"Oh, it's pretty simple, Skye," Max said, expression deadly earnest. "I love you. I think I've been in love with you from the moment I came back here and saw you coming down the sidewalk in that flowered sundress you were wearing. You looked like a goddess."

All right, this had to be a dream. Maybe I'd dozed off on the sofa instead of heading out to Max's, or maybe....

Because if this was real life, I would have thought of something stunning and eloquent to say to him in response to his declaration of love, instead of just sitting there and staring at him, mouth open, like a fish caught on a hook.

Somehow, though, I found my voice. "Why—why didn't you say anything before this?"

"Because I could tell you just wanted to be friends," he replied. "And I tried to tell myself that was okay, that it was better to have you in my life as a friend than not at all. I actually was maintaining pretty well until I saw you with Calum at the Coyote Cantina. Because it was one thing if you were single, but something else completely different if you were dating someone."

Part of me wanted to laugh. All this time, I'd been desperately trying to be Max's friend and nothing more, figuring that was what he wanted, while he'd thought my casual attitude was a clear indication I wasn't interested in anything more than a continuation of our childhood friendship.

It was harder than I'd thought it would be to meet his gaze squarely and not blink, to pray he'd be able to see some of the hope and need reflected in my eyes. But I knew I needed to say it. I needed to make sure he knew how I felt.

"Max, I've been in love with you my whole life," I said quietly. "When you came back, I thought all you wanted was friendship, so I tried to act that way. If I'd known—if you'd said even a single word—"

That was as far as I got, because Max rose from his chair, came over to where I sat, and practically lifted me from my seat, his fingers twined in mine, his head bending so our mouths could meet.

He tasted of sangria and smelled faintly of some kind of cologne or aftershave, a little spicy, warm and friendly, just like him. As soon as our lips touched, it was as if my entire body came alive, heat rushing through me and tingling at the same time, all the way down to my toes.

That kiss went on for what felt like an eternity. At last, though, he pulled away just a little, as though he needed to gaze down at me and make sure this really was what I wanted, that we hadn't been at cross-purposes yet again.

Oh, I wanted this. Every single cell in my body was telling me how much I wanted it.

"Wow," I whispered, and he shot me a relieved grin, those happy crinkles around his laser-blue eyes making me melt all over again.

"So...I guess that was okay."

"Much more than okay," I told him.

Still smiling, he leaned down to kiss me once more, only this time his arms wrapped around me so he could pull me close, so I could be pressed up against his lean, muscled body. Heat flared again, and I held on for a long time, not wanting to let go.

But even the best kiss in the world has to end sometime. I heard an embarrassed cough from somewhere behind me, and I let go of Max...only to see Lou, one of his bodyguards, standing a yard or so away and doing his best to stare down at a particularly interesting paving stone at his feet.

"Um, sorry, boss," he said. "I just wanted to ask if you wanted me to make some Texas toast to go with your steaks."

Unlike me—I could tell my cheeks were flaming with embarrassment—Max sounded easy enough as he said, "Texas toast sounds great. Thanks, Lou."

A nod, and then Lou—who was about 250 pounds of no-nonsense Sicilian—fled the scene, presumably so he could hide in the kitchen.

Eyes still twinkling, Max looked down at me. "Well, I don't know about you, but I've sure worked up an appetite."

Despite my worries about Calum's tragic and untimely death, that was probably one of the best nights of my life. Max and I had steaks and skewers of marinated mushrooms, and Texas toast and corn on the cob, all washed down with a gorgeous zinfandel he'd picked up the last time he was in Santa Fe. All during dinner, we talked about the lengths we'd gone to in order to conceal our feelings for each other, and how silly all those efforts had turned out to be in the end.

"And yet you went out with Justin Hale," Max said, wearing a sly grin.

"Only because I thought I needed to move on with my life," I returned, waiting while he poured another half-inch or so of wine into my glass. "Believe me, I suffered agonies of guilt over the whole thing...and that was way before I found out he was a stone-cold killer."

Max's expression sobered a little. "It still scares me what a close call you had with that guy. If Kyle hadn't mowed him down—"

"But he did," I cut in, and reached across the table so I could place my hand on Max's free one. "Nothing happened."

"No, but not for lack of that bastard trying."

Well, that was true. If Kyle hadn't come around the corner in his squad car at exactly the right moment, I honestly didn't know what would have happened.

Oh, boy...Kyle. As happy as I was to be sitting here with Max, to realize that all my wistful dreams really had come true, I really didn't want to think what Kyle's reaction was going to be once he found out that Max and I were a couple.

Well, tomorrow was Sunday. Unless we had the extreme bad luck to bump into Kyle while we were coming out of the bail bondsman's or something, I figured we could put off that fraught moment until at least Monday, maybe later.

"Justin's safely locked up, awaiting trial," I said. "For now, I think we need to concentrate on getting Mason Fowles out of jail and trying to figure out what the heck really happened to Calum."

"You don't think it was natural causes?" Max asked. He gently let go of my hand, but only so he could pick up his steak knife and cut another piece of perfectly medium-rare rib-eye.

"No. I don't know what happened, but there's more to this than a simple heart attack. Otherwise, I really doubt that Chief DeVargas and the D.A. would have tried to charge Mason Fowles with murder."

Max nodded, telling me he was willing to go along with my whims for now and see where our investigations took us. Because even though he hadn't come right out and said it, I knew he wanted to be with me as I did my best to figure out what really had gone down in Calum's room at the Plaza Hotel.

And I was just fine with that. After so many years of living separate lives, I wanted to make sure Max Sullivan was at my side as much as possible.

The evening ended with Max walking me to my car and promising he'd be over around ten the next morning. We both seemed to agree that, as incendiary as our kisses had been, it was probably better to wait a little, to not immediately hop into bed just because we'd declared our feelings for one another at long last.

Exactly how long we'd be willing to wait was an entirely different question.

Since we hadn't finished the bottle of zinfandel, I figured it was safe to drive home. The streets were quiet, the skies clear, unshrouded by any thunderclouds. The whole night seemed to shimmer around me, the streets and landmarks I knew even with my eyes closed appearing as if they had some kind of magical glow to them.

It wasn't really there, of course. No, this was just the afterglow of those kisses with Max, of realizing he loved me just as much as I loved him.

Could the world be any more beautiful?

Of course, I was brought back down to earth when I walked into the house, since Tilly was sitting in the middle of the living room, her tail waving back and forth.

"I don't see the point in you having me come over here when you're not even around most of the time," she groused.

That remark seemed just a little unfair, considering I didn't go out all the time, and in fact spent a good chunk of my weekends puttering around the house, cleaning, doing laundry, handling all the other little tasks I never seemed to have time for during the week.

But I could tell trying to point out that very basic truth wouldn't win me any points with the cat, so I only said, "It's to make sure you get properly fed, remember?"

"I did perfectly well on my own back before you started bringing me to your house for the weekend," Tilly shot back.

I set my hands on my hips. "Okay, fine. Since my spell to keep you from talking to anyone besides Deanne and Max and me seems to be holding, I suppose there isn't any reason to keep having you here. Is it okay if I drop you back downtown tomorrow, or do you absolutely have to go tonight?"

Tilly's tail waved back and forth again, telling me she probably wasn't too happy that I'd called her bluff. However, she just said, "Tomorrow is fine," and stalked off toward the kitchen...and, I guessed, the cat door I had installed there.

In fact, I heard it smack shut a moment later, letting me know she was going on one of her evening rambles around the neighborhood. I wasn't a huge fan of those constitutionals, even though it had been years since anyone had seen a coyote in the immediate vicinity and she was in much more danger from a motorist going over the speed limit.

But she'd spent plenty of time roaming around downtown before I cast that spell to make her talk, so I was probably worrying over nothing.

It wasn't very late—a little after nine—and yet I figured I might as well get ready for bed. Settling in to watch something on Netflix or Hulu seemed horribly anticlimactic after the revelations of earlier tonight.

Besides, Max and I were going to get Mason Fowles out of jail tomorrow, and I had no idea what might happen after that. Best to get my sleep now while I could.

Just as I was about to turn out the light on my nightstand, my phone pinged.

Max.

I wanted to say goodnight since I'm not there to tuck you in. Missing you already & can't wait to see you tomorrow morning. Love you.

My heart did a flip-flop. Even though I'd heard

him say those words only a few hours earlier, seeing them written out like that thrilled me right down to my fingertips.

Love you, too, Max.

I sent the message, then pressed my phone against my chest for a moment, probably looking like some lovestruck high school kid who'd gotten the first text from her crush.

What would the fifteen-year-old me have thought of everything that had happened in my life this evening?

She'd probably think she was dreaming, I thought, and smiled.

Well, sometimes dreams came true.

CHAPTER 10

Flying the Coop

A quick text exchange with Darcy Montoya had given me the names of two local bail bondsmen who were mostly reputable. Only one of them was open on Sunday, though, so his office was where Max and I headed after grabbing breakfast at Charlie's near downtown.

I have to say going out to eat that morning was kind of a production, mainly because Max insisted we didn't need to hide the shift in our relationship and that we might as well be open about the situation. While part of me wanted to shout to the whole world that Max Sullivan was in love with me, my more cautious side couldn't help thinking it might be a good idea to keep things on the down-low, if only for a short time.

Max prevailed, though, and that was why we ended up sitting next to each other in our booth rather than across from one another. And although he didn't try making any gratuitous public displays of affection, it was probably obvious to anyone looking at us that no one who wasn't involved in some way would have been squished that close to their breakfast partner.

No one said anything, though—to my infinite relief—and we left the restaurant full and happy. I had no doubt that as soon as we were out the door, the people who'd seen us together there would be texting their friends to tell them the news.

Well, my fellow Las Vegans were gossips, and there wasn't much I could do about that. They weren't malicious about it, though, and only liked to share the town's latest news with anyone they thought would be interested.

However, it seemed obvious as soon as we set foot inside Security Bail Bonds that the man sitting behind the desk there definitely hadn't heard about how Max Sullivan, Las Vegas's most prominent citizen, had finally decided to make it official with his long-time friend. He looked like he was maybe in his middle or late fifties, thickset but not fat, with thinning gray-streaked dark hair and matching gray-frosted brows.

"Help you?" he said.

At once, Max stepped forward. "We're here to post bail for someone being held at the police station."

"Name?"

"Mine or the prisoner's?"

"Prisoner's," the man said curtly. Voice still flat, he added, "I know who *you* are, Mr. Sullivan."

Max's self-confident stance seemed to deflate a little, but he managed to say, "His name is Mason Fowles. He was arraigned on Friday, June sixth."

The man turned his attention to the computer in front of him, typed in something, and nodded. "Got him right here," he said. He glanced past the computer screen, brows raised slightly. "That's a pretty hefty fee. You do know you won't get your fifty thousand back, right?"

"He won't?" I broke in. Somehow, that particular little detail about posting bail had slipped by me.

"No, I won't," Max said, now sounding cheerful. "That's how these guys make their money. But I'd rather risk fifty K than the entire half million, just in case your instincts are totally wrong about this one and Fowles decides to take off for Mexico, or whatever."

I really didn't see that happening, if for no other reason than Mason Fowles would stick out like the proverbial sore thumb if he made a run for the border.

"You're sure?" I said in an undertone. "It's still an awful lot of money."

Max took my hand and gave my fingers a quick

squeeze. "Totally sure. If this is the quickest way to solve this mystery, then I'll consider it money well spent."

He still sounded way too upbeat, but I had to remind myself that his concept of money and mine were worlds apart. To him, that fifty thousand dollars probably didn't feel like anything more than my last hundred-dollar splurge at the Ulta beauty store in Santa Fe.

Smiling, he pulled a checkbook out of his back pocket. "I hope a personal check is all right. Banks aren't open today."

"A personal check will be fine," the man behind the desk said. Tone dry as the hot summer day outside, he added, "It's not like I don't know where to find you."

"True enough."

After taking a pen from the cup on the bail bondsman's desk, Max wrote out the check, then tore it off and handed it over. The man studied it for a second, nodded, and tucked it into a drawer.

"I'll send the bail electronically," he said. "The station should have a record of it in the next half hour or so. After that, your guy will be free to go."

Perfect. I thanked him—even as I couldn't help thinking that was a pretty nifty way to earn fifty thousand dollars for a few minutes' work—and Max and I went outside.

"A half hour," I said as we buckled our seatbelts

and he started up the Bronco. Wonderfully cool air started gushing out the vents, and I let myself lean against the seat back. "What should we do with that time?"

"I can think of a few things," he replied with a grin.

So could I, but I definitely didn't want our first time together to be a quickie in between a visit to a bail bondsman and springing Mason Fowles from jail. "Well, I suppose we can go downtown and wander around for a bit," I said.

Being Max, he didn't look at all deflated by my suggestion. For all his success and ambition, he was still one of the most easygoing people I'd ever known. "Works for me," he said as we pulled away from the curb.

Less than ten minutes later, we were parking on Plaza Avenue, not too far from the police station but not in its proper lot. It would have felt strange to take one of their spaces when we wouldn't be conducting business there for another half hour or so, and it wasn't that far to get from there to the hotel. Darcy had told me that Mason's personal effects were being stored at the police station, since he'd lost his room at the Plaza after his arrest.

Remembering all the suitcases and trunks he'd been hauling up to his room the first time I'd seen him, I had to wonder where they even had room for all that stuff in the station. An evidence locker room, I supposed; it wasn't as if they arrested enough people on any given day that the space would already be full.

"Actually, I have an idea," Max said as soon as we stepped out of his Bronco. "There's a painting I've been eyeing in the gallery down the street. Let's go and take a look at it, and you can tell me if you think buying it is a good idea."

I sent him a sideways glance. "Max, I don't know anything about art."

"No," he said easily, "but you did a great job remodeling your house, and I figure you can tell me if it's a good fit for my place. Back in L.A., I had an interior designer who took care of all that stuff for me."

He seemed supremely confident that I'd be able to give him the same help here, even though I had absolutely no credentials beyond watching a lot of home improvement shows and cherry-picking the designs and elements I thought would work best to bring my old farmhouse-style home into the twenty-first century.

Then again, he was only asking my advice on one painting, not getting my input as to whether he should knock down a wall or something.

"Okay," I said. "Sounds like fun."

His blue eyes twinkled down at me, and once again, I experienced a hot rush of need. What was it about him that could make my knees turn to rubber and every cell in my body think of nothing except Max Sullivan?

Well, I supposed that was the knock-on effect of being in love with the guy since I was just learning to read and write.

Luckily, the gallery was open, probably to take advantage of any weekend visitors who might like to bring home something more permanent from Las Vegas than just a T-shirt or a beer cozy.

Lorraine Evans, the gallery owner, was standing behind the antique table she used as a desk. She smiled at the two of us and said, "Good morning. Just let me know if there's anything you have any questions about."

"Will do," Max replied genially, then led me toward the rear of the gallery where the larger paintings were displayed.

I followed him, knowing I felt way more conspicuous than I actually was. By this point, Max had been living in Las Vegas for nine months, and people were completely used to catching glimpses of him out and about, and even seeing him in my company, considering the way we'd grab a bite sometimes or meet at Byron T's for drinks when neither one of us felt like hanging out at home.

All the same, I couldn't help wondering whether something in my aura had changed, whether it would look as though I had a big flashing "I kissed Max Sullivan" sign hanging over my head. Nothing in the way Lorraine had greeted us gave any indication that she knew about the shift in my status from friend to...well, I wasn't sure what Max and I were, except that our relationship definitely wasn't platonic anymore.

Looking relaxed and casual as he always did, he stopped in front of a large painting, one with a simple wood frame that added to the piece without drawing too much attention to itself.

"What do you think?"

I could see why he'd been drawn to this particular painting. Done with oils in an unfussy, almost *plein air* style, it depicted the golden, rolling hills outside town, with a line of lush cottonwood trees along a river bottom and some billowy monsoon clouds in the background. In fact, I had to wonder if those trees were the same ones that bordered Max's property, because the scene was almost identical.

"It's gorgeous," I said truthfully. The piece evoked a late summer day pretty much perfectly, and would be a spectacular addition to Max's house. "I think it would be perfect on that big wall in the living room, the one where you have the mirror right now."

He practically beamed. "That's exactly where I was thinking of putting it. I just wanted to get your opinion before I made the plunge."

The little plaque next to the painting named the artist and the title of the piece, which was "Summer Vantage." It also listed the price—almost ten thousand dollars.

Of course, that was chump change to someone like Max, but still, I was kind of glad he'd hesitated to buy the painting until he knew for sure it was the right one. It told me he was still careful with his money.

For the most part, that is. I couldn't forget the way he'd casually written that check for fifty thousand dollars to the bail bondsman only a few minutes earlier.

However, I had a feeling Max had only done that because getting Mason Fowles out of jail was something I wanted. Otherwise, he would have been a lot more cautious.

"It's perfect," I said honestly.

"Then let's buy it."

I couldn't miss the way he'd said "let's," as though this was a decision that affected both of us.

Was he already envisioning a future where we would be living together?

I wanted to believe such a thing was possible... but I also knew it was kind of crazy to go there when all we'd done so far was share a couple of kisses and have breakfast together.

Lorraine came over, probably because she'd guessed we'd had enough time to look at the painting and didn't want to let it go too long in case she missed out on a sale. "Is that the one you're interested in?" she asked, trying not to sound too hopeful as she nodded toward "Summer Vantage."

"Yep," Max said cheerfully. "It's great. Is it all right if I buy it now and then have someone come over tomorrow to pick it up for me?"

"That'll be fine," she replied. Once again, I got the impression she was trying to keep herself from doing a happy dance right then and there. It wasn't as though she made a big sale like that every day of the week.

I guessed that Max would send Lou or Al—or maybe both of them—to the gallery tomorrow to fetch the painting for him. While technically they were supposed to be his security detail, it definitely seemed to me that Max had them do all kinds of little odd jobs...not that they appeared to mind too much. Now that the paparazzi had decamped, it wasn't as though he needed 'round-the-clock bodyguards.

And it made sense not to be lugging some over-sized painting along when we went to spring Mason Fowles from jail. It would probably fit in the back of Max's Bronco if he put the seat down, but then Mason wouldn't have anywhere to sit.

I hung back a little while Max pulled out a black Amex card and handed it over to Lorraine, who wrote up a sales slip for him. "I'll put a 'sold' sign on the painting," she said. "We're open eleven to five tomorrow, so come by whenever works best for you."

"Will do," Max said, sliding the receipt into his wallet. "Thanks, Lorraine—have a great day."

Oh, Lorraine was having a very good day, that was for sure.

That business handled, Max and I headed back outside. He squinted up at the sun, as if gauging how much time had passed, then said, "You think it's okay to go spring Mr. Fowles now?"

"Probably," I replied. "Only one way to find out, though."

He grinned and slid his hand into mine as we began to walk toward the police station. Just feeling the pressure of Max's fingers and knowing he was fine with such an open gesture of affection in such a public place made me that much happier. Clearly, he didn't care if the whole world knew we were together.

Still hand in hand, we entered the police station. I didn't recognize the woman working at the front desk, probably because I'd never had any reason to be there on a Sunday. From time to time, I'd drop off any leftover muffins or other pastries at the station rather than have them go to waste, but that only happened Monday through Friday.

The deputy recognized Max right away, but I'd long ago gotten used to that flash of surprise in people's faces. She was older than either one of us, probably in her early forties or so and therefore someone who might not be as much a member of the Max Sullivan fan club, but she still put up a hand to smooth her hair and then straightened slightly.

"Can I help you?" she asked.

"We just posted bail on one of your prisoners," Max said, casual as though he'd done this a hundred times before. "Mason Fowles."

"Let me check," the woman said. The badge she wore identified her as Deputy Lopez, although she hadn't bothered to introduce herself. She typed something into the computer, then nodded. "Yes, his bail has been posted. Wait here, and I'll bring him out to you."

I found myself relaxing a little at those words, as if some part of me had still feared we'd be thwarted somehow when we got to the station, that maybe the money transfer had gotten bogged down somewhere.

That didn't seem to be the case, though, and a couple of minutes later, Deputy Lopez returned with Mason Fowles in tow, a duffle bag slung over one shoulder. He wore a frown and didn't seem especially happy to see either Max or me, but maybe that was just because he'd had to spend one more night in jail than he'd hoped.

However, he did at least mutter, "Thank you,"

as the deputy undid his handcuffs and told him the conditions of his bail required him not to leave town unless given permission by the judge. That admonition made his scowl deepen, but he didn't say anything, only followed Max and me out of the station.

Once we were standing on the sidewalk, though, he crossed his arms and said, "Why'd you post my bail?"

Max shrugged. "Because Skye asked me to."

Maybe I spotted the slightest flicker of surprise in Mason's pale eyes, as though he couldn't quite figure out how an ordinary person like me would have that much influence with a celebrity like Max Sullivan. However, he didn't ask any other questions, but only said, now sounding like his usual irritated self, "The deputy only let me take this one bag. She said I'd have to come back tomorrow to get the rest of my things because they don't have a full staff on Sundays and she can't leave the desk to get it all out."

"That's fine," I said quickly. "You can make do for one night with what you have, and then we'll make arrangements to get the rest of your stuff out of hock sometime tomorrow." I paused there, realizing that, although we'd gotten Mason out of jail, we hadn't really made any plans as to what we should do with him once he was free. "Do you want to go back to the Plaza?"

His lips thinned. "I don't think I'm very welcome there."

No, probably not, since he'd been hauled out of the place in handcuffs. I glanced over at Max. "Should we take him to the Castañeda?"

"I don't know," Max replied, sounding dubious. "It's owned by the same company, so he might be *persona non grata* there, too."

"Well, you can always leave me on the side of the road," Mason snapped.

Somehow, I resisted the urge to roll my eyes.

But then Max grinned. "I've got the perfect place. He can stay in the casita at the ranch."

For a second, I stared at him, startled that he'd make such an offer. True, I often forgot Max's property even had a casita, since it was a good distance away from the main house and we never had any reason to hang out in that particular guest space, but still it seemed kind of crazy that he'd be willing to let Mason stay there until his trial.

On the other hand, it might be just about the perfect solution. The casita was completely self-contained, had two bedrooms and a small kitchen and a bathroom. If Mason was staying there, he wouldn't be in Max's way, but he'd also be following the judge's orders to stay in town. Right on the edge of town, but still.

"'Ranch?" Mason repeated, sounding dubious.

"Max's property on the east side of town," I

said. "The casita is really nice, and you could have some privacy there."

A second or two passed while Mason appeared to mull over the offer. "I suppose it'll have to do," he said ungraciously. "Where is it?"

"We can drive you there," Max offered, but Mason shook his head.

"My car is still parked down the street. I'll follow you."

So we ended up all climbing into Max's Bronco, and then drove the couple of blocks to the spot where an ancient Suburban was parked on a side street around the corner from the Plaza Hotel. Mason signaled that it was his, and Max pulled over while the other man got into his vehicle. At first, it didn't seem like it wanted to start, but eventually the engine turned over, a puff of smoke belched out the tailpipe, and he laboriously pulled away from the curb as Max started rolling again.

"This is awfully nice of you," I said as we began to head east away from downtown.

He shrugged. "We had to put the guy up someplace, and the casita is a lot nicer than the local Best Western, or whatever. Besides, he's less likely to get into trouble out there. I'll have Lou and Al go pick up his stuff tomorrow when they come to get my painting." Max paused there, a wry grin tugging at his lips. "You think I'm crazy, don't you?"

"No," I replied, and leaned over so I could press

a kiss against his cheek. He hadn't shaved that morning, was deliciously scruffy, and I could feel the faint sting of his stubble against my lips. "I think you're possibly the nicest guy on the planet."

Max laughed outright at that comment, although he kept his eyes on the road. "There are some people in Hollywood who might have a slightly different opinion of me. But I'll take it."

I somehow doubted that. Everything ever written on the subject of Max Sullivan seemed to make a point of telling everyone what a nice guy he was, generous and definitely lacking the kind of *prima donna* attitude you might expect from someone with his kind of fame.

"So," I said, "does this mean you're going to get stuck babysitting Mason Fowles?"

Max angled a glance at me, then returned his attention to the road. "Did you have something in mind?"

"Well, I was kind of hoping I could make dinner for you—if you didn't have any other plans, of course."

Another smile, and he said, "Nope, no plans. And I've got Lou and Al to keep an eye on Mason and make sure he doesn't get into any trouble, so I'm pretty sure I can slip away for an hour or two."

Thank God. It had already been brewing in the back of my mind that I should have Max over for dinner, that it would be nice to have a quiet, intimate evening for two someplace far away from any prying public eyes. True, Tilly would be there, but since she wasn't really interested in people food unless she was digging it out of a trash can, I had a feeling she wouldn't stick around for the meal.

And now that I knew Max's security team could keep watch on Mason, I wouldn't have to worry about him slipping a monkey wrench into my plans.

"Perfect," I said. "Can you come over around six-thirty? I have to eat kind of early because it's a work day tomorrow."

In answer, he reached over and gave my hand a quick squeeze. "Six-thirty is great. That means I won't have to wait as long to see you again."

Happy little warmth bubbled up in me again. No, I wasn't any closer to finding out who—or what—had killed Calum McRae, but at least Mason was out of jail, and Max seemed to be more than happy with the way things currently sat between the two of us.

I'd just have to hope that eventually, the answer to the mystery would reveal itself.

CHAPTER 11

Some Enchanted Evening

We got Mason settled in the casita—he still seemed cranky about the whole thing, but was slightly mollified to realize the guest house was bigger than most two-bedroom apartments, and definitely much nicer than his room at the Plaza Hotel—and promised him we'd fetch the rest of his belongings as early on Monday as we could.

"And I'll have Al run to the store and get you whatever you need for meals," Max promised.

"That will be difficult," Mason replied. "I'm vegan and have to be careful about what I eat."

Of course he was. The diet explained his lean physique, though, and after both Max and I pointed out that the local Walmart had a surprisingly good plant-based selection, Mason seemed to back off a little, saying he'd put together a list.

With that handled—and after he'd warned Al

he was going to have to go shopping later that afternoon—Max drove me home. I knew I'd have to do some shopping of my own to make the dinner I had in mind, but I didn't say anything about that.

No, I wanted this meal to be a surprise.

We kissed before I got out of the car, and when he asked what kind of wine to bring, I only said, "Something fun and Italian."

"We're having Italian food for dinner?"

I shrugged. "Just bring a nice sangiovese or whatever."

That comment earned me a grin. "Ah, okay... you want to be all mysterious. I can work with that."

"See you at six-thirty," was all I said, and he shook his head, still smiling, as I shut the car door.

Once I was inside my house, I went straight to the kitchen so I could get out one of my cookbooks. This wasn't the first time I'd made pasta carbonara, of course, but it had been a while, and I wanted to make sure I didn't forget any of the ingredients when I headed over to Walmart in a bit.

However, I'd only started to make my shopping list when my phone rang.

Calling so soon? I thought as I picked it up.

That wasn't Max, though. No, it was Deanne's number displayed on the iPhone's home screen.

I didn't even get a chance to say hello, though,

because she immediately screeched, "When were you going to *tell* me??!"

"Tell you what?" I responded, even though I had an inkling as to why she was calling. Only a few topics would have been important enough to make her pick up the phone during her second honeymoon.

"About you and Max!"

"How'd you find out about that?" I asked. All right, I knew exactly how—Las Vegas's trusty grapevine—but still, the exact details of the information filtered through to my best friend should be interesting.

"My mom's friend Evelyn saw you and Max at Charlie's this morning, and she called my mom to ask her if she knew that you and Max were dating. My mother said she didn't know anything about it, so she called me to see if I knew what was going on." A pause so she could take a breath, and Deanne added, "What, were you just going to wait until I got back to fill me in?"

"I didn't want to bug you during your vacation —" I began.

"This isn't 'bugging' me," she retorted. "It's letting me in on an extremely important development. So...what happened?"

Boy, where to start. As quickly as I could— mostly because, even though Deanne didn't seem to have any problem with spending as much time on the phone with me as necessary, I didn't want to throw a complete monkey wrench into whatever her and Mike's plans for the day might be—I told her about Calum coming to Las Vegas, and how the time he and I had spent together seemed to have made Max finally realize his true feelings for me.

"This whole thing with Calum is just awful, though," I concluded. "That's why I'm trying to figure out what really happened. And Max is helping."

"Of course he is," Deanne replied. "I could tell he's been wanting to play Hardy Boy to your Nancy Drew for a while now."

"But which Hardy Boy?" I asked, and I could hear her chuckle.

"I have no idea," she said. "I think I only read one or two of those books when I was a kid, so I can't even remember their names."

Actually, neither could I. The important thing, though, was that Max wanted to be a part of my investigation, and didn't think it was silly or something that should be left to the authorities.

Of course, considering my track record solving crimes compared to the local police department's accomplishments when it came to apprehending murderers, I could see why he might feel that way.

Deanne and I chatted a bit longer, and then she told me she needed to go. "I can't believe we're going to be here for five more days," she groaned. "I'm missing out on *everything!*"

"Are you seriously complaining about being on vacation in Hawaii?" I asked, only half joking.

A pause. "Okay, I guess I am," she admitted with a small chuckle. "But it's just so typical that all this is happening while I'm thousands of miles away."

I reassured her that I'd fill her in on anything she might have missed during her absence, and then we said our goodbyes and ended the call.

A glance at the clock on my stove told me I still had plenty of time, but I knew I needed to get to the store soon if I wanted everything to be ready and perfect at six-thirty when Max came over.

Time to get to work.

The dough for the garlic bread was starting to rise, and I'd tidied up the living room and set the dining room table. I wouldn't actually put the sauce together until closer to Max's arrival, which meant I had a little time to kill.

Should I attempt another tea leaf reading?

As soon as that thought went through my mind, I promptly shot it down. I was already keyed up, wanting to make sure this evening was flawless in every way. I doubted I'd be able to concentrate and get any kind of a true reading.

But there was something else I could try.

I went up to my office and spent another fruitless twenty minutes trying to crack the password on Calum's laptop. No matter what I tried, though, no matter the combination of letters and numbers, the thing stayed stubbornly locked. Once again, I had to wonder if Kate McRae had known what she was talking about when she said her brother wasn't too concerned with computer security, because right now, the contents of that MacBook Air felt as though they'd been hidden in a vault in Fort Knox.

This was starting to get really annoying.

As I closed the lid and secured the laptop in the bottom drawer of my desk, though, I wondered if there was something else I could try, something I might have missed.

Exactly what, I had no idea.

But then I thought of how Mason still had to get most of his personal items out of hock, and that led me to think about the belongings Calum had left behind. Kate had said she was making arrangements to have his body sent back to California, but what about his luggage? Was she having that shipped, too?

What if there was something he'd left at the hotel that could help me get into his laptop?

It was not quite five. Pretty soon, I'd have to head back down to the kitchen to finish the rest of the meal prep, but for now, I had a few spare minutes.

I'd brought my phone with me to my office, so I entered my passcode and then found the phone number for the Plaza Hotel. There was a slim chance that Pedro Montaño might be working the front desk, since he also covered weekend shifts for any hotel employees who needed the time off. Even if it wasn't Pedro who answered the phone, most of the people who worked there knew me and would probably be able to answer some of my questions.

To my relief, though, I recognized his voice as soon as he picked up the phone. "Plaza Hotel, how can I help you?"

"Hi, Pedro," I said. "It's Skye. I was wondering if you could help me out with something."

"Sure," he replied, although his tone altered just the slightest bit and now sounded almost guarded. I had a feeling he was wondering if I was going to ask to poke around in Calum's room and trying to figure out what he should say if I did make such a request.

However, I hadn't planned to ask for anything nearly so intrusive. "What happened to Calum McRae's stuff? Are you holding it somewhere?"

"No," Pedro replied immediately, sounding much more relaxed. "His sister asked us to box it up once the cops were done going through everything. A guy from UPS picked it up yesterday afternoon."

Well, darn. I'd really been hoping to have a chance to go through his things. Even though I was feeling a little deflated, I made myself ask, "Do you remember if you saw any notebooks or papers or anything like that?"

Because I'd been hoping that maybe Calum had written the really important stuff out longhand somewhere, figuring it was impossible to hack a notebook. If that turned out to be the case, then maybe I wouldn't need to get into his laptop at all.

Unfortunately, Pedro said, "No, nothing like that. Just clothes and his phone, toiletries, that kind of stuff."

I supposed it was possible Calum had been keeping duplicate notes on his phone, but since I knew it would be even harder to get into—mostly because I'd get locked out after a few tries—I wouldn't allow myself to be too depressed over the realization that his cell phone, along with all his other personal effects, was already getting trucked... or flown...back to California.

"Oh, okay," I said. "Thanks for letting me know."

"It's no problem," Pedro responded. He hesitated for a second or two, then added, "This whole thing is kind of a bummer. We had a couple people cancel after they found out about what happened to him."

While I had a feeling Calum's death was a one-off event, I couldn't really blame people for feeling a little hinky about staying at a hotel where one of the guests had apparently been frightened to death.

"I'm sorry," I said. "I'm trying to figure out what really happened. I'm pretty sure it didn't have anything to do with the Plaza's ghosts, though."

"Hope you're right," Pedro said. "Gotta go—have a good one."

"You too."

We ended the call there, and I set my iPhone down on my desk. So far, I hadn't learned anything remotely useful.

Also, I didn't know if it was entirely the truth that the hotel's ghosts hadn't been responsible for Calum's death. Up until recently, they'd been more mischievous than anything else, but what if they'd decided it was time to stop playing around and instead go after the one person who was trying to unearth their secrets?

I didn't like that idea at all.

But I told myself there had to be a completely logical reason for everything that had happened, even if I didn't yet know what it was.

Now, though, I needed to get down to the kitchen and back to work.

The Plaza Hotel's ghosts would have to wait, because Max was coming over for dinner.

"This all looks amazing," he said as he surveyed the spread on the dining room table. In addition to the big bowl of pasta carbonara, there was also home-made garlic bread, and salad with vinaigrette dressing and grape tomatoes I'd picked from the plants in my garden just an hour earlier. Blue eyes warm with admiration, he added, "And you look amazing, too."

A happy flush spread to my cheeks. Because I knew he liked the teal flowered sundress I'd worn last summer when we first reconnected, I'd put it on now, along with some pretty strappy sandals with low enough heels that I knew they wouldn't prevent me from putting all the finishing touches on the meal after I got dressed.

"Thanks," I said, knowing how awkward I sounded. I'd never been very good at accepting compliments. "But go ahead and sit down."

I'd told him to take the place of honor at the head of the table, so he sat there now, while I settled myself in the seat to his right. As promised, he'd brought over some Italian wine—not sangiovese, but a luscious-looking montepulciano.

He uncorked it now, then poured a little into

my glass and into his. "I can think of about a million things I want to toast to," he said.

So could I. But Max's and my future seemed bright with or without a toast, while Calum's had been cut abruptly short. "Let's drink to finding out what really happened to Calum McRae."

The smile Max had been wearing faded, and he gave a single nod. "I think that's a good toast."

We touched our glasses together, and each of us had a swallow of the wine he'd brought. It was amazing, but that didn't surprise me very much. Among all his other sterling qualities, Max Sullivan was awfully good at choosing wines.

The solemn moment passed as I dished some salad for both of us, and he picked up the basket of bread, took a piece, and then handed it over to me. "Maybe someday I'll get used to the way you do this so effortlessly," he remarked after he had a bite of salad. "You're sure you didn't use some magic to get all this put together?"

"None at all," I said primly, although I kind of ruined the moment by cracking a smile. "Well, unless you count the way I levitated to get my big mixing bowl off the top shelf."

"That sounds like magic to me."

I just shrugged and ate some salad as well. Although the magic from the Petrucci side of the family could be super-powerful, I'd done my best to avoid using most of it. However, levitating to get stuff off high shelves didn't seem like too much of an abuse of my powers, and I had to admit it did come in handy an awful lot of the time. When I'd remodeled the kitchen, I'd made sure to have the cupboards go all the way up to the nine-foot ceilings. It looked great, but if you didn't have magic to propel you up to those tippy-top shelves, it meant a lot of dragging step stools around.

"Deanne called," I remarked after I'd had another sip of montepulciano. "She was very put out that she's missing all the excitement."

Max shook his head and swirled some pasta carbonara around his fork. "I suppose I can see that. I got the feeling she was rooting for you and me to get together, even if I was too dense to realize back then that you wanted the same thing."

"We were both dense," I said, which was only the truth. How many months had we wasted doing this silly dance around each other, both of us thinking the other person wanted to be friends and nothing more?

Way too many. But I wasn't going to give myself too much grief over our shared blindness. As my grandmother had liked to say, everything happened for a reason. Maybe it was important that Max and I had gotten together now, and not the moment he'd gotten back to town. If nothing else, it showed that we worked well as friends, too, that this wasn't some animal chemistry thing and not much more.

Speaking of chemistry, I couldn't quite ignore the effect he had on me just sitting there, the way our eyes would meet every once in a while. I knew he was fine with taking things slow if that was what I wanted...but right now, I realized that was the exact opposite of what I already knew in my heart.

We'd been in each other's lives for years. What was the point in waiting now?

All the same, I tried to keep the conversation casual, letting him know I still wasn't having any luck getting into Calum's laptop and how I'd called the hotel in the hope that some of his belongings would still be there. And Max went along, telling me how Al had brought back a huge haul of vegan goodies for Mason, although he hadn't seemed too appreciative.

"Still," Max went on, "it looks like the guy's going to be okay there for the meantime. He's got plenty of food, and the casita has wi-fi. I also told him he's free to walk around the property as he likes, but to keep in mind that I've got video security all along the fences."

"I'd think he'd like that," I commented. "At least he won't have to worry about anyone trying to sneak up on him."

Max's mouth curled in amusement. "To be honest, I'm not sure that guy actually 'likes' much

CHRISTINE POPE

of anything. But whatever. He's taken care of and has someplace safe to hole up, and that's probably as much as we can do for him right now."

"All the more reason to find out what was going on with Calum," I said. "Because once we get that figured out, then the D.A. will drop the charges, and Mason can go back to Tucson and get out of your hair."

"Amen to that."

The two of us clinked wine glasses again, and he poured a little more wine into my glass and then his. I sipped, knowing I was getting just a teeny bit tipsy despite all the food I'd eaten. However, it was early in the evening—the world was still light past the curtains, even though I'd closed them all and lit candles, hoping to create a more romantic mood.

Or...considering the way Max looked at me right then...maybe the candles hadn't been necessary.

I cleared my throat. "Hope you left room for dessert. I made tiramisu."

His eyes met mine, hungry despite the second helpings he'd had of everything. A corner of his mouth lifted as he said, "I think you know what I want for dessert."

A delicious little thrill stole through me. I knew exactly what he was talking about, because I wanted the same thing.

Without replying, I lifted the napkin from my

lap and set it down on the table. Max echoed those movements, then stood.

I really didn't know who stepped forward first. Not that it mattered, because in the next moment, we were kissing one another, tasting the wine on each other's tongues, bodies pressed together.

And then we were hand in hand, hurrying up the stairs, leaving the dishes on the table to be collected later.

We went into my room and closed the door, even though, as I'd predicted, Tilly had been nowhere to be found during our entire meal.

Then I wasn't thinking about the cat or anything except the reality of Max, the feel of his lips against my throat...the realization that here, now, was the only thing in the world that was of any real importance.

Afterward, he murmured, "I love you," and I snuggled against him, knowing that whatever else happened, I'd never been so happy in my entire life.

CHAPTER 12

Get Your Ghost On

Of course, reality settled in soon enough... right after I realized this had all been wonderful, amazing, but I still had to get up at four-thirty the next morning.

"I don't mind," Max said. "I can sleep through just about anything."

Maybe he could. But I still didn't like the idea of having to leave him sleeping here while I headed off to work. If nothing else, I didn't have a spare key I could give him.

Well, that, and as much as I loved him, as much as I knew that our lovemaking had sealed something important between us, I still wasn't sure whether I was ready to have him see me in all my awful o'dark-thirty glory, with bedhead and zero makeup.

"No, it's better if you go on home," I said. "I

don't want to subject anyone to my work schedule. We can see each other after I'm off work."

For a moment, he was quiet, as if trying to decide whether it was worth arguing the subject further. Apparently, he realized he shouldn't push on this particular point, because he said, "Okay, I get it. But we're definitely going out tomorrow night. Smoky Joe's okay?"

Smoky Joe's was the new smokehouse restaurant that had opened on Bridge Street about a month earlier. It was one of the projects slated to be on *Fix My Town,* but after they lost both their producers—one as a murder victim and the other as the murderer himself—the production company had closed everything down. It was only because Max had come in and paid for all the projects' completion out of his own pocket that the restaurant had opened at all.

I'd heard that the Mackenzies, the owners, had tried to make Max a silent partner as a way of saying thank-you for his contribution, but he'd demurred, saying he just wanted to help out and make sure their business was a success.

Which it definitely was. Las Vegas didn't have any other restaurants which offered that kind of food, so they were packed pretty much all the time.

Even so, I knew we wouldn't have any trouble getting a table. The Mackenzies might not have been able to have Max as a silent partner, but I had a feeling they'd instructed their hostesses to make sure he always got a prime table no matter how busy the restaurant might be.

"Smoky Joe's is perfect," I said.

Max kissed me again, and another thrill went through me. It was kind of amazing how much I wanted him, considering we'd already spent the better part of two hours in one another's arms.

"You're sure you don't want me to stay?" he whispered.

Of course I wanted him to stay. But I also had a business to run, and I had a feeling some of my saltier patrons wouldn't be too thrilled to miss out on their morning's coffee and muffins just because I'd spent the greater part of the night before getting spectacularly laid.

"Don't make me answer that," I said with a grin. "Just get going before I change my mind."

He smiled at me in return, but only reached over and squeezed my hand. "Okay."

By that time, I'd wrapped a robe around myself and he was fully dressed, so I walked him downstairs, kissed him again, and then shut the door and locked it before I could lose my nerve. And even though it was definitely an anticlimax...to say the least...I made myself clear off the table and put the leftovers in the fridge, although I knew I wasn't going to bother with rinsing the plates and setting them in the dishwasher.

Right after I turned out the lights and just as I was about to climb back up the stairs, Tilly's voice came to me in the darkness.

"If those are the sorts of activities you're going to be engaging in from now on, then there's no way I'm staying here on the weekend," she snapped.

I turned. Since she was a black cat and the room was dark, I couldn't see much of her except a faint green gleam where her eyes caught the illumination from one of the sconces on the landing.

"Sorry to disturb your beauty sleep," I said.

She let out a small hiss. "It was very disruptive," she replied. "I could hear you all the way down the stairs even with your door shut."

Well, we had been pretty vocal. Good thing all the windows had been closed and the A/C compressor outside had been humming away, doing its best to fend off the early-summer heat.

But I refused to be embarrassed, not when I'd just had the best night of my entire life. "Then be glad we already decided that you can stay at the store most weekends," I said sweetly. "And now, I need to get to sleep."

Tilly made a sound that seemed suspiciously like a "hmph," but she didn't say anything else.

Thank God for that. If I couldn't have Max here with me, then I was going to pitch face-first into bed and sleep like the dead.

I almost thought someone would have to notice there was something different in my appearance or attitude the next day, but if any of my patrons had detected a certain glow about me, they kept their observations to themselves. Which was fine. I counted some of them as friends more than customers, and yet I still didn't think I wanted to be discussing my love life with them.

A little after two, Leila Moreno came into the shop for her customary go-cup of green iced tea. She looked tired, and when I asked her if everything was okay, she only gave a fatalistic shrug.

"It's okay," she said. "But the ghosts have really been off the hook ever since Calum McRae died."

"Really?" Not that I'd spent a lot of time at the Plaza Hotel after that fateful night, but I hadn't noticed anything particularly strange when I went in there to talk to Pedro.

Leila sipped some of her tea before replying, as though she needed that extra little jolt of caffeine to muster the strength to reply. "Yeah. Lots of banging on the walls, although the manager keeps insisting it's just the pipes. But I've worked there long enough to know what's pipes and what's ghosts. Also, Abby swears she keeps seeing that little girl ghost down by the service elevator. She's so creeped out, she won't even go down there anymore. She makes me go instead."

"Have you seen the ghost?" I asked.

Another shrug. "Nope. I mean, sometimes it feels as if there's something moving right at the corner of my eye, but when I turn around to look, there's nothing there. In a way, I think that's worse than seeing the ghost outright."

I had to admit it all sounded pretty unsettling. "What are you going to do?"

"I don't know," she said, one corner of her mouth drooping in the beginning of a frown. "It's a decent job because the tips are good. But if things don't get better soon, I might have to start looking for something else. I heard maybe one of the waitresses at The Skillet is thinking of moving to Albuquerque. If she leaves, then I might apply for her job. At least that place isn't haunted."

No, it wasn't. Or at least, I'd never heard of any specters loitering around the popular burger joint. Like a lot of places in Las Vegas, the building that housed the restaurant was old, but it didn't appear to have come with its own complement of ghosts.

Leila brightened a little then, saying, "Maybe you should go down to the basement again and try to talk to them."

Oh, hell no, I thought. However, refusing her request outright when she seemed so stressed didn't feel very kind, so I only replied, "I tried that. It didn't work."

"But were you *really* trying to talk to them?" Leila persisted. "I thought you and Calum were only down there taking measurements or whatever."

Well, true, it wasn't as though we'd gone to the basement to play ghost-whisperer or something like that. And I honestly had no desire to return if I could help it.

"I don't communicate with spirits," I told her. "Sure, I read tea leaves, but that's something entirely different. It sounds to me as if the hotel managers should try to find someone who specializes in that kind of thing."

Leila didn't quite snort, but the derisive sound she made definitely got her point across. "Like they'd do anything like that," she said. "They don't even want to go on record and say the place is haunted, especially now that it's costing them reservations. But you—you're some kind of psychic, even if you don't want to admit it. And you're local. I think the spirits would respond better to you, since you're not some stranger."

Would that even make a difference? I didn't know much about the spirit world, but it seemed to me that either you were dead, or you weren't. Where you'd come from when you were alive really shouldn't matter very much.

"Let me think about it," I said, which was about all I felt safe offering right then.

Even so, that equivocal answer seemed to cheer Leila immensely. Her dark eyes brightened, and she said at once, "Oh, if you could go down there and talk to them, I really think it would help a lot."

"Well, I'll see if maybe Max can go with me," I replied. "Because I know there's no way I'm going back down there by myself."

"Whatever works," Leila said, obviously undeterred. "But I need to get back to work. Just let me know if you decide to go to the basement."

"I will."

She hurried out, and I tried not to sigh. Even though I'd told myself there was no way I'd ever return to that haunted space, somehow Leila had managed to talk me into it, despite all my maybes and "thinking about it."

Sounded like I was going to be doing a lot more than that.

"Sure, I'll go with you," Max said.

We were sitting in a nice little corner booth at Smoky Joe's, tucked away from the crowds. Even though every table in the restaurant was occupied, it didn't seem as if anyone was paying much attention to us, which was exactly how I liked it.

"Really?" I asked as I reached for my glass of rosé. "You don't think it's a bad idea?"

Max considered my question for a moment. "Not really," he said. "I mean, it seems pretty obvious that all the activity is generating from that one spot, and if the ghosts really are acting up the way Leila says they are, then we should probably try to find out what's setting them off. I'm no psychic researcher or anything, but I also don't scare easily."

No, he didn't. I honestly had a hard time visualizing Max Sullivan afraid of much of anything. He was smart enough to back off when he knew he couldn't prevail in a particular situation, but I couldn't think of anyone I'd rather have watching my back.

"So...when?"

The waitress came by with our food—a pulled pork sandwich for me and a brisket platter for Max—which meant he had to wait to reply until she'd set down the plates and told us she'd be back to check on us in a little bit.

"No time like the present," he replied, and I stared back at him.

"You mean...after dinner?"

"Sure," he said easily. "I mean, we both agreed on only one drink tonight because you have to work tomorrow, and the hotel is right down the street. Might as well take a look while we're both here."

On the surface, his suggestion made some sense. As he'd just pointed out, we were already downtown, and it wasn't like either of us was going to be impaired by drinking a bottle of wine or anything.

Still....

"Do you think it's okay for just the two of us to do this, though?" I said. "Maybe we should go get Mason Fowles and bring him along. After all, he has a lot more experience with this kind of thing than either of us. Last time, I had Calum with me."

That suggestion made Max raise an eyebrow. "Do you really think the staff at the Plaza Hotel is going to be happy about having a guy who was accused of murder in their hotel just a couple of nights ago coming back and wandering around in their basement?"

Well, when he put it that way—

"Okay, maybe not," I said hastily.

"Besides, it's not as if you haven't been down there before," Max added. "You know what to expect."

Yeah, and that's exactly why I'm not super thrilled about having to head back, I thought, although I figured I should probably keep those sentiments to myself.

"All right," I said, doing my best not to sigh. "We'll go check it out after dinner."

Neither Leila nor Abby were working that night, but Pedro was on duty at the front desk.

"Sure, if you really want to go down there," he said. "It's been pretty quiet today, though."

I chose to take that bit of information as a good sign. "What were the ghosts doing before now?"

"Oh, the usual," he replied with a small lift of his shoulders. Maybe Leila had been freaked out by the ghosts' increased activity this week, but he didn't seem too worried about it. "Knocking on walls, footsteps in empty rooms. A cold spot here and there. Luckily, everyone who's staying here right now either thinks it's cool or just blows it off and blames it on the plumbing or something."

Yes, that was lucky for them—I supposed all the scaredy-cats had already headed for the hills, or at least our town's Best Western.

Then again, I probably shouldn't be calling those particular tourists scaredy-cats, since at the moment, I would have been all too happy to take off for less haunted spaces as well.

But because Pedro had given Max and me the go-ahead, there wasn't much we could do except make our way down to the basement.

This time, we went through the lower level of the lobby, past the restrooms, and down the sloping corridor that led to the basement door. Even though Pedro had assured us it was unlocked, I half expected there to be some resistance when Max pushed on it.

The door opened easily, however, and I reached out to flick the switch on the wall just past it, turning on the yellowish overhead lights. Their watery illumination wasn't the most reassuring thing in the world, but it was definitely better than blundering around in there guided by only the little flashlights on our phones.

Even though I'd been down here before and maybe should have been the one to take the lead, Max obviously didn't intend to put me on the spot like that. He slipped his hand into mine and said in a murmur, "Where did you find those initials?"

Intensely reassured by the pressure of his fingers against mine, I replied in an equally low voice, "Over there."

We walked to the spot on the brick wall where I'd seen those two initials only a few days earlier. In a way, it was hard to believe such a short time had elapsed, because on that previous occasion, I'd been standing here with Calum, not Max, and hadn't even known the man who accompanied me now loved me just as much as I loved him.

I wanted to think that love surrounded and

protected us now, but I also knew the world of ghosts and spirits didn't always work that way.

"Here," I said, pointing at the wall.

Max let go of my hand so he could dig his iPhone out of his pocket and shine it on the wall. Some part of me had been worried that the marks might have disappeared, that they might have been left there by a mischievous ghost to mess with me, but no, the small "A.M." stood out clearly against the aged plaster, even in the dim lighting.

Because the initials were so far down on the wall, he had to squat to get a closer look at them. "Do you have any idea who left these?" he asked.

"No," I replied. "I think that was something Calum was trying to find out, but if he actually managed to dig up any useful information, it must be on his laptop."

That damn laptop. Once again, I wanted to kick myself for my utter failure in having any luck at getting it unlocked. True, cracking passwords wasn't exactly my field of expertise, but still.

Then Max froze. "Over there," he said in an undertone.

Although he didn't exactly move, his eyes shifted, the whites showing as he looked off to our extreme left, where the boiler had once stood and now only patched brick wall remained.

Standing near the corner was the little ghost girl. I knew she couldn't be real because I could see the texture of the wall behind her, the alternating squares of aged brick and pale mortar. Despite that, the detail on her dress was much more obvious than it had been in my dream, even though she still appeared in shades of grayish-sepia. It had short puffed sleeves and detailed smocking on the chest in a light gray that I guessed had been pink in real life, matching the pale band of satin ribbon in her dark hair, which fell in the same corkscrew curls I'd seen in my dream.

Her eyes were big and dark as well, sad in a way I couldn't quite describe but recognized even across the decades that separated us. She pointed at the initials at the wall, then inclined her head.

"Is that you?" I asked. No, I didn't have any idea of how to be a true medium, but it seemed obvious enough to me that the little girl wanted to talk to us.

No real response at first. Her delicate little brows lifted, and then she shook her head.

Was she trying to tell me those initials weren't hers, or was she only trying to communicate that she couldn't hear me, could only see my lips moving?

I had absolutely no idea.

Max's hand stole into mine. His grip was warm, if a little tight, telling me that, while he might be having a hard time with all this, he had no intention of bolting.

In fact, he spoke then, gaze fixed on the ghost girl. "Did your name start with 'A?'" He pointed at her with his free hand, then traced a capital "A" in the air in front of him.

At once, her pretty little face lit up, and she nodded. Her lips moved, but of course there was no sound.

Still, I thought I could tell what she was saying.

Sí, sí.

I could already tell she was Hispanic, and the way she'd responded in Spanish rather than English told me she had to have been from one of Las Vegas's numerous Latin families, many of whom had been here long before New Mexico was a part of the Union...in fact, long before the thirteen colonies had become the United States.

Then she blinked out of existence. No gentle fading away, just here one minute and gone the next.

"Holy crap," Max breathed.

That about summed it up. "So, those are her initials," I said, and smiled up at him. It might have been only a tiny piece of the puzzle, but that was all right. That one clue was more than we'd had a few minutes earlier. I added, "Now we just have to figure out who she was."

CHAPTER 13

Sticky Fingers

Naturally, all Max and I could talk about after our trip to the basement was the ghost. He drove me home, but he didn't just drop me off. No, we went inside and I got some chilled water with lemon for both of us so we could sit down in the living room and decide what to do next.

"If she died young, there's got to be some record of what happened to her," Max said.

Unlike the other times he'd come over before we'd declared our feelings for one another, this evening we were snugged up against each other on the couch. He felt big and solid and reassuring, so, even though we'd communicated with a ghost only ten minutes earlier, I didn't feel too worried about our encounter with the spectral plane.

I sipped some water, then shook my head.

"Not necessarily," I said. "Kids died young back then a lot more than they do now."

Max frowned a little as he considered my words. Almost immediately, though, his expression turned sunny again. "Maybe, but there's got to be some connection between her and the hotel, or she wouldn't keep showing up there. Maybe she died in the boiler explosion."

I'd wondered the same thing, even though I had to believe that if the little girl—and maybe the boy who was often spotted with her, even though we hadn't seen him tonight—had perished in the explosion, there must have been some record of it. After all, dying in such a spectacular way wasn't the same thing as passing away from diphtheria or whatever else might have claimed too many young lives back in the early 1920s.

The early 1920s....

I sat up straight, and Max looked at me in surprise.

"What is it?"

"I think I know why the ghosts have been so active lately," I said. Briefly, I told him about the dream I'd had, about how it definitely looked as though the scene had taken place sometime in the 1920s. "Judging by their clothes, that would make it about a hundred years ago," I went on. "What if the appearances of the ghosts in the basement are surging now because we're coming up on the hundredth anniversary of their deaths?"

Max's eyes lit up, and he leaned over and gave me a quick kiss. "You're positively brilliant, Skye," he said. "I'm sure that's it. Now we really need to find out when that boiler explosion took place, and who it took with it. What's the best way to do that?"

Because I'd already learned that details about Las Vegas's history—well, the more obscure stuff, and not the things pretty much everyone already knew—were hard to track down on the internet, I knew we didn't have a lot of avenues to explore. Calum had mentioned researching some things at the library, but I had to believe there was only one other venue he could have gone to after that if the answers he was looking for continued to elude him.

"We need to visit the historical society," I said. "They're the only place I can think of that would have the information we need."

"Okay, we'll go tomorrow morning," Max responded at once.

He was looking so excited that I hated to bring him back down to earth. Still, I knew there was no way I would have the time to go anywhere until I closed up shop at three-thirty.

"In the afternoon," I said gently. "Remember, I'm flying solo this week, so I don't have Deanne to cover for me the way I usually would."

His expression abruptly deflated. But then he summoned his usual brilliant smile and said, "Oh, right. Well, that's okay. I've actually got a Zoom call with Margaret tomorrow at eleven, so I would've had to be home for that anyway."

A call he probably could have rescheduled if I really had been available to go over to the historical society as soon as they opened. Still, I was glad he would have something to occupy at least part of his time while I was at work.

"You can come to the shop right at three-thirty," I told him, hoping to myself that I wouldn't have any last-minute customers who might delay my departure. "We'll head over after that. I think the historical society is open until four, but we should probably check their hours just in case."

After I made that comment, Max pulled his phone out of his pocket and did a quick search. "Yep, ten 'til four Monday through Friday." He stopped there, now looking a little concerned. "Do you think a half hour will be long enough for us to find anything useful?"

"If it's not, we'll just come back again the next day," I said. "But we can talk to Dorothy Innes, who runs the place, and see if she'll let us stay just a little bit longer if necessary."

This piece of news made Max plant another kiss on my cheek. "Is there anyone in Las Vegas you don't know?"

I couldn't help smiling. "Oh, a few. But Dorothy usually comes in and gets a hot chocolate in the winter and an iced tea in the summer on her way to work, so she's definitely one of my regulars."

"It's a plan, then." Max stopped there, his expression growing uncharacteristically serious. "Are you sure you don't want me to stay over?"

Well, of course I did. But it didn't seem very nice to do that to him when I had to get up so early in the morning. "We talked about that already," I said. "Weekends, sure. But I don't want to inflict my schedule on you."

"I really don't mind."

No, he probably didn't. It wasn't as though I had any intimate knowledge of his sleeping habits, but I got the feeling he was the kind of person who could just immediately roll over and go back to sleep even when woken up at some ungodly hour. If nothing else, it would be a good skill to cultivate when dealing with all the offbeat hours he had to keep while working on set.

So, maybe my reticence had more to do with avoiding the uncomfortable scenario where one of his parents might see him strolling out of my house the morning after, and not quite so much any worries about costing him his beauty sleep. While the Sullivans had been great neighbors—and friends—to me all these years, I wasn't sure how they would react when they figured out their son's relationship with the girl next door had morphed into something way beyond simple friendship.

"You didn't even bring a toothbrush," I joked, and his blue eyes twinkled at me.

"You're right—I didn't. So, if I come back tomorrow night with a toothbrush and some clean underwear, does that mean I can stay?"

How I could I resist that adorably lopsided smile, the teasing glint in his eyes? I was already weak-willed enough around Max Sullivan to begin with, and now—

"Okay," I said. "Tomorrow night."

He leaned over and kissed me, a real kiss this time, and I was more than happy to put aside any worries about ghost girls and visits to the historical society so I could lose myself in his embrace.

At times like this, he was the only thing that mattered in my world.

About an hour later, we kissed goodnight and promised again to meet at Levitation Latte at three-thirty. I stood on the porch and watched him walk down the path, then get in his Bronco and drive away. For all I knew, one or both of his parents had witnessed his departure, but since it was only a little past nine o'clock, his leaving at that hour didn't feel as incriminating as it would have if he'd left at seven in the morning, even if we might have participated in basically the same activities either way.

I locked the door and headed upstairs. As I passed my office, though, I thought maybe I should try working on the laptop for a little bit. Yes, I was already up past my bedtime, but ten minutes or so wouldn't make much of a difference, especially since I felt wide awake and not quite ready to go to sleep.

After turning on the light, I headed over to the desk and opened the bottom drawer where I'd hidden the laptop after the last time I'd tried to hack its password.

It wasn't there.

Alarm flared at once, even as I told myself that I'd been kind of distracted lately, what with everything that had been going on between Max and me. Maybe I'd put the laptop in a different drawer.

However, a quick search of the drawers big enough to hold a MacBook Air told me it wasn't in any of those places, either. And even though I knew there was no way I would have stuck Calum's computer in my file cabinet, I went ahead and rifled through its contents as well.

The laptop wasn't in the closet, or shoved under the armchair I had in one corner.

No, as far as I could tell, that damn thing had disappeared right into thin air.

Panic wanted to shrill along every nerve ending, although I tried to reassure myself that even if someone had come in here and stolen the laptop, it wasn't as though they'd be able to get much from it.

Unless they have the password, I thought.

Which was ridiculous. No one in Las Vegas would have known Calum's password. I doubted it was the sort of thing he shared with anyone; clearly, his sister hadn't known it, or she wouldn't have left the little MacBook with me in the hope that I might be able to crack the code.

Of course, even if the actual contents of the laptop were safe for now, that didn't get me past the extremely troubling fact that someone had broken into my house while I was out with Max.

The front door hadn't been tampered with, as far as I could tell. My key had gone into the lock without any trouble, and had turned smoothly as well.

But I hadn't checked the back door....

Heart pounding, I hurried downstairs. As I went through the house, I kept looking around me, trying to see if there was any evidence of any items being moved or taken. Everything seemed to be exactly where it needed to be, which meant...what? That the intruder hadn't been a simple burglar, that they'd come in here expressly to take the laptop?

I didn't like that idea very much. For one thing, who else even knew I had Calum's MacBook?

That list was a pretty short one. Pedro Montaño, of course, but why would he have any reason to take the laptop in the first place?

None that I could think of, although I didn't dismiss his possible involvement out of hand.

Max, but he'd been with me all night, and again, if he'd wanted the laptop for some strange reason, he could have just asked to borrow it.

Then I froze. No, I hadn't said anything in front of Mason Fowles, but what if he'd somehow figured out that Calum's laptop hadn't been sent back to California with the rest of his belongings, and had instead stayed here in Las Vegas with me? After all, I'd been helping Calum with his investigation, so that kind of leap of logic wasn't completely unbelievable. Also, Mason had his own car over at Max's ranch, which meant it would have been all too easy for him to drive over to my house while Max and I were out having dinner.

Not sure what I was going to find, I went to the back door. It was closed but not locked.

Which meant...what? That someone had picked the lock?

Or had I just forgotten to lock it the last time I went out into the yard? I suddenly remembered I'd been hurrying earlier that day, wanting to go out and water the plants, which had been wilting in the scorching heat. It was possible I'd been in such a rush that I hadn't stopped to turn the deadbolt.

After all, it wouldn't have been the first time I'd left the back door open. My town was pretty safe, and while there was the occasional car break-in or some other kind of property theft, it was very rare in my neighborhood. No, my street had always been the kind of place where you could leave your unlocked car in the driveway or even your front door standing open—like my neighbor Lucy Margolis had done once or twice—and not have to worry about anything going missing.

So...maybe I'd been broken into, and maybe I hadn't. I supposed I could have called Kyle to have him come over and dust for fingerprints or something, but if it really was Mason who'd come over here and taken the laptop, I doubted he'd be sloppy enough to not wear gloves or simply wipe down anything he'd touched after he was done.

No, it wasn't Kyle I needed to call right now.

I sighed, then got out my phone.

Either way, it didn't look as though I was going to get a lot of sleep tonight.

"I did not steal that laptop!" Mason Fowles protested.

Max and I exchanged a glance. After I'd called him and explained to him what was going on, he'd told me to come over—and to pack an overnight bag.

"No way are you staying in that house by yourself if someone really did pick the lock," he'd said.

"And if it was Mason?" I'd asked.

"I'd still rather have you close by," Max had replied without missing a beat. "Lou's on duty tonight. I'm pretty sure he could twist Mason Fowles into a pretzel without breaking a sweat."

Well, that was true. Mason might have five or six inches on the guy, but Lou was big enough that he could probably bench press the ghost hunter.

Which was why Max and Mason and I were all sitting in Max's living room at nearly ten that night, with Mason perched on the edge of an armchair and looking positively feral with rage.

"I did not take that laptop!" he growled. "I was here all evening. I never left the casita."

"Well, *someone* took it," Max returned calmly.

Mason flicked an irritated glance in my direction. "Maybe they did, but that person was not me. I was on my own laptop at the precise time you're talking about. You can check your wi-fi logs if you don't believe me."

Now it was my turn to look over at Max. I

supposed it was possible to look up that sort of thing and determine whether anyone had been using data on the home's network during a particular period, but I was darned if I knew how to go about doing such a thing.

However, Max surprised me by saying, "That's easy enough. You two hang out here for a minute."

He got up from where he was sitting on the couch next to me and left the living room, presumably to go down the hall to the ranch house's office. That left me to stay there alone with Mason Fowles, a situation I would have preferred to avoid.

"You know I didn't do it," he said, still looking like he wanted to launch himself from the chair and flee the room.

Honestly, if he wanted to continue protesting his innocence, he should really have learned not to look so guilty. "I don't know anything for sure," I replied. "I just know that only a couple of people even knew I had that laptop, and three of them are at this ranch right now."

This comment didn't seem to earn me many points. Now Mason's eyes narrowed even further behind his wire-rimmed glasses, and he sniffed. "Then you should be talking to that man at the Plaza Hotel," he said. "Not me."

Maybe so, although I still couldn't think of any reason why Pedro would want to take Calum's laptop. Also, I had a pretty good idea that he was at work right now, and therefore would have a water-tight alibi even if we did decide to turn our suspicions in his direction.

Max came back a few minutes later, expression almost downcast. "It checks out," he said as he sat back down next to me on the sofa. "There was a lot of data moving around from the port in the casita, and it wasn't Lou or Al, because they were using their phones during that time." He looked over at Mason. "What were you doing, downloading porn?"

I wanted to giggle, but Mason appeared even more self-righteously annoyed. "Of course not," he said. "I was watching a YouTube video about a haunting investigation in Vermont. You can check my history on the channel, if you want."

Because he'd been so quick to offer that information, I had to believe it was the simple truth. Max must have come to the same conclusion, because his shoulders lifted and he said, "All right, you didn't take it. But if that's the case, you don't mind if I poke around in the casita, do you?"

Mason's expression told me he did mind, very much, although he didn't protest. "If you must."

The three of us trooped out of the house and down the hill toward the spot where the casita was located. A low quarter-moon hung in the western sky, and the air was sweet with the scent of sun-baked grass, lingering long into the evening. It was the sort of night where I would have loved to sit out on the patio with Max, sipping some sangria, enjoying each other's company.

Instead, I was out poking around some lunatic ghost hunter's crash pad.

To be fair, the little house was neat and tidy, and indicated that Mason was showing the place some respect, even if he wasn't entirely happy about being stuck here in Las Vegas. The bed, covered in a striped quilt in shades of blue and rust and gold, was made, and the only thing really out of place was the laptop sitting on top of the round oak table in one corner.

"You see?" Mason said as he stalked over to the laptop. "YouTube."

When he opened the lid, it showed a paused video of a darkened scene in what appeared to be an old house, even though the lighting was bad enough that I couldn't exactly tell what was going on. Still, it looked innocuous enough.

Max only nodded, then went and peered under the bed, opened the drawers in the dresser one by one, and turned on the light in the casita's dressing area so he could inspect the closet as well. When he was done, he came back to where I stood, disappointment clear in every angle of his posture.

"There's nothing here," he said.

"I could have told you that," Mason snapped.

"You'll need to look elsewhere for your thief. And now, if you don't mind, I'd like to go to sleep."

"Sorry," Max said. "We had to check."

"I am sorry about this," I added, but Mason seemed unmoved.

"Good night," he said, although his tone seemed to indicate he wished exactly the opposite for us.

Since there wasn't much else to say, Max and I headed outside, and Mason slammed the door as soon as we left the casita.

"Well, so much for that," I remarked. "Now what?"

Max took my hand and pulled me toward him, and kissed me under the light of the moon. However, that seemed to be the only romance in the cards for the remainder of his evening, because he said, "Now, you go to sleep. You're already up way past your bedtime, young lady."

Yes, I was. And if the two of us hadn't already stolen some time together earlier tonight, I might have made more of a protest.

As it was, I said meekly, "Okay, Max," and he laughed and led me toward the house.

The mystery of the missing laptop would have to wait for another day.

CHAPTER 14

Past Mistakes

I didn't sleep as well as I might have liked, but it didn't really matter. Even if I'd been up all night, I still would have had to pry myself out of bed and go to work. And that wasn't just because Deanne was out of town—she was great at making coffee, but baking still eluded her, and the most she could manage was to take batter I'd already made and use it to bake the shop's muffins. If she'd had to do it from scratch, she would have been hopelessly lost.

Although I was generally okay with just one cup of coffee, that morning I had two before the shop even opened at seven o'clock. The extra jolt of caffeine was enough to make me mostly functional, although I had the feeling it was going to be an extremely long day.

My own house was locked up tight, so I wasn't

too worried on its behalf, especially since it seemed pretty obvious to me that the thief had only been concerned with taking Calum's laptop and nothing else. And even though I'd had to tiptoe out of Max's house at a little past 5 a.m., Al had already been there to deactivate the security system and walk me to my car. Everything had seemed quiet as I left; I doubted we'd awakened Max, who was sleeping in the master suite on the other side of the house, but still, slipping away in the early morning darkness like that had only served to increase my current feeling of unreality.

What exactly was going on here? Why had the little ghost girl been so intent on making sure we knew she was the "A.M." who'd scratched her initials on that wall?

I didn't know. And unless we got really lucky at the historical society this afternoon, I had a feeling Max and I would be probing the mystery for days to come.

But all thoughts of ghosts and spirits were chased away as soon as the morning rush began at seven, and I really didn't get a chance to come up for air until close to eleven. In a way, that was good, just because it did help to focus on work and nothing else.

When Kyle came in at around eleven-thirty, I'd already eaten the ham and cheese croissant I'd tucked away for my lunch and was feeling reasonably better about life. Still, seeing him put me immediately on my guard, and the first words out of his mouth didn't help the situation much.

"So, you and Max bailed out Mason Fowles," he remarked. "What the heck were you thinking?"

"That he wasn't guilty," I said. "Muffin? Or would you rather have a croissant?"

"A croissant and some iced tea, please," Kyle replied, which was sort of out of character for him, since he usually had a muffin and coffee.

Then again, it was an awfully hot day. We hardly ever hit a hundred around here, but on this particular June day without a cloud in sight, it sure looked as though Las Vegas was going to try for a record.

I got a croissant out of the case, poured Kyle his iced tea, and asked, "Do you want any butter or jam for that?"

"No, I'll have it plain."

It wasn't until he'd eaten a few bites of the croissant and drunk some tea that he seemed ready to pick up the conversation again. "You really think Fowles isn't guilty? The guy's a complete tool."

"True," I agreed. The ghost hunter definitely hadn't won any brownie points with me, that was for sure. "But being a tool doesn't make you a murderer."

Kyle absorbed my comment for a moment as he chewed another bite of croissant. Then he seemed to push that topic out of the way and went on to something he obviously considered a lot more important.

"So...you and Max are a thing now?"

There it was. Considering the way news got around in town, I supposed I shouldn't be too surprised that Kyle had found out about the progression in Max's and my relationship. All the same, I'd kind of been hoping in the back of my mind that the gossip wouldn't have reached Kyle's ears quite yet.

"Um...yes," I replied, since there really wasn't any way to dodge the question. "We've been spending a lot of time together, and...."

I let the words trail off there, since I was starting to get into delicate territory, and I really wanted to do whatever I could to avoid hurting Kyle's feelings any more than they already had been. Yes, I could tell myself until I was blue in the face that we hadn't been together for more than a year, so it definitely wasn't as though I was cheating on him or anything, and yet...

...and yet, it probably never felt good to discover that the woman you still carried a torch for had decided to transfer her affections to someone you could never possibly compete with.

"It's okay," Kyle said. His tone was casual enough, although I could tell from the tension in his jaw and throat that it was definitely less than okay for him. "I kind of knew you'd always been in love with him. I guess I just hoped you'd be able to move on."

I think I blinked. "You *knew?*"

He shrugged and picked up his go-cup of iced tea. "Maybe not in so many words. Just a gut feeling, sort of. Anyway, congratulations...I guess."

Somehow, I managed to smile. "I don't think congratulations are in order just yet. It's still kind of early days for us."

"Maybe," Kyle said, sounding dubious in the extreme. "Anyway, I need to get going. Thanks for the snack."

He picked up his go-cup of tea and headed out. While he had his head high and he looked brisk and calm enough, I could tell he definitely wasn't happy.

I released a breath and told myself I shouldn't feel guilty. Kyle and I had broken up long ago. It wasn't as though I was cheating on him with Max.

Except...back when Kyle and I had been together, I sort of had. Not physically, of course, since Max was a thousand miles away in Los Angeles at the time, but still, my mind and my heart had always belonged to him, no matter how far from me he'd been, no matter who else I was with.

Maybe someday I'd figure out the right way to apologize to Kyle for all that.

I had a small rush around lunchtime, and then another, oddly, at two, which kept me occupied enough that I didn't have much opportunity to brood over that exchange with Kyle. Not for the first time, I wished I had more true girlfriends in Las Vegas, someone I could fix him up with.

The only two viable candidates I could really think of were Darcy Montoya and Leila Moreno, and Darcy really wouldn't have been a good choice because of the way she and Kyle both worked for the police department. I didn't know for sure whether or not the Las Vegas P.D. had rules about that sort of thing, but it still was probably better for them to look elsewhere. Besides, if Kyle was into her at all—assuming there weren't any regulations forbidding it—you'd think he would have asked her out already.

And Leila—well, I liked Leila, but I didn't know whether their personalities would mesh all that well, despite my suspicions that she thought he was cute. Also, they both worked crazy hours, which would make it that much harder for them to even try dating.

I knew my own schedule was kind of crazy, too, but at least it was consistent. Getting up so early wasn't much fun, and yet I knew I never had to worry about working on the weekend or late at night. Also, I probably could have shifted my hours just a teeny bit and opened at seven-thirty instead of seven, but I didn't know whether that extra half-hour would have made much of a difference in my day-to-day routine, so I'd left it alone.

And then it was three twenty-five, and Max came into the shop, looking cheerful and tanned and as though he'd just jetted in from St. Tropez or something, in his khaki shorts and pale green linen shirt.

Had this godlike creature really decided to fall in love with a mere mortal like me?

Apparently, he had, because he bent and kissed me full on the mouth, tasting sweet and minty, as if he'd had some gum or brushed his teeth before heading over to pick me up.

"How was work?" he asked.

"Fine," I said. "Nothing much to report."

I paused there, wondering whether I should hide that exchange with Kyle from Max. Then again, the last thing I wanted was for us to be keeping secrets from each other.

Better to get it out in the open.

"Kyle came in," I went on. "He was kind of surprised that we'd bailed out Mason Fowles."

"I myself question the wisdom of that decision," Max remarked with a grin. "That guy's a real Suzy Sunshine."

I couldn't help grinning. "Yes, his people skills

could use some improving."

"Also, he hasn't been much help with this whole ghost-hunting thing," Max added, to which I sent him some serious side-eye.

"I seem to remember suggesting that he come to the basement at the hotel with us and totally getting shot down."

"True," Max agreed, looking undaunted. "And I stand by that decision. I'm pretty sure his negative energy would have chased off any ghost in a fifty-mile radius. No wonder Calum was kicking his butt on the ghost-hunting front."

At Max's mention of Calum, my smile slipped a little. He'd died four days earlier, and we still weren't any closer to finding out who—or what, I had to admit—had frightened him so much that he'd expired on the spot.

Well, with any luck, we'd be able to figure out something soon.

I untied my apron. "Let's get over to the historical society."

Dorothy Innes was about my mother's age, but the two women couldn't have been more dissimilar. Alicia Petrucci looked at least ten years younger than her real fifty-two, with long dark hair and big brown eyes just like mine, while Dorothy was one of those women who appeared as though she must have been born wearing a sweater twin set and with her hair in a bun.

The twin set was in place now, even though the temperature outside—according to the dashboard thermometer in Max's Bronco, anyway—was a searing ninety-eight degrees. The air conditioning in the historical society building was surprisingly powerful, though, maybe because of all the old books and papers inside that had to be kept at a consistent temperature.

"The boiler explosion?" she said in answer to my question, and frowned. "Yes, that was in the early 1920s, but I can't remember the exact year. Let me go check on that for you."

She disappeared through a door at the rear of the historical society's main room, a prim little place with black and white photos of Las Vegas in days gone by on the walls, and several light oak tables with matching chairs at the center of the space, presumably where visitors could sit down with choice documents from the archives and peruse them at their leisure. Dorothy's desk sat about five or six feet in front of the door she'd just exited through, a large oak piece with a luxuriant African violet sitting to one side. I had to think she'd placed the desk in exactly that spot so there'd be no chance of a patron getting past her to rifle through her precious archives.

Max looked around the space, a small smile playing around his lips. "You know, I've never been here before, but this place still looks exactly like I pictured it."

I couldn't help grinning. "Well, considering Dorothy's been in charge here since we were in grade school, I guess it's not so strange that it's kind of preserved in amber, so to speak."

That comment broadened his smile, but he didn't have a chance to reply, because Dorothy returned right then, a green file folder in one hand.

"Yes, I thought the explosion was covered in the local paper," she said. "June 13, 1923."

That revelation made me shoot a significant glance in Max's direction. June thirteenth was only a few days from now, meaning that the hundredth anniversary of the boiler explosion was almost upon us.

No wonder the ghosts had been getting restless.

He gave me a very faint nod. "Do you mind if we take a look at the paper?"

"Not at all," Dorothy replied. "You can sit at one of the tables here."

Under her eagle eye the whole time, but that was all right. It wasn't as if Max and I planned to abscond with her precious newspaper clippings. No, we just wanted to see what the reports of the day had to say about the disaster that had occurred at the Plaza Hotel a hundred years ago.

Max thanked her as she handed over the folder, and the two of us took a seat at the table farthest from her desk. She'd still be able to see everything we were doing, but at least over there we'd have a chance to talk as long as we kept everything at a low murmur.

He pulled out a chair for me—the unconscious chivalry might have surprised some people, but I knew Max was just like that—and then sat down himself before opening the green folder. Inside were stacks of clippings neatly paper-clipped together, organized by week.

Back in the 1920s, it seemed, the local paper was content to print the news weekly rather than daily. Actually, it had gone back to a weekly rag about five years ago after it nearly went out of business, so I suppose you could say the Las Vegas *Herald* had merely returned to its roots.

The green folder contained clippings from May and June 1923, so it took Max a minute to locate the article we were looking for. But soon enough, he extracted it from its stack after carefully removing the paper clip, then laid it out flat so we both could take a look at its contents.

Plaza Hotel Suffers Boiler Explosion! proclaimed the headline, which was in a big, black font. Underneath, the article explained how the boiler under the hotel had experienced some kind of valve malfunction, leading to a buildup of pressure that eventually resulted in the explosion that had damaged portions of the basement. From the way it was described, it sounded as though the hotel was lucky not to have been completely leveled by the blast.

The article went on, *It is with extreme sadness that this writer must reporter that Antonio Moreno of Las Vegas, 62, died in the explosion. The hotel manager has stated that Mr. Moreno was in the basement of the property, attempting to diagnose the problem with the boiler, when the blast occurred. He leaves behind his oldest son, Pablo, his daughters Catalina and Margarita, and his grieving widow, Maria. Funeral services are pending an examination by the local coroner's office.*

That was all, and I looked up from the paper, a frown creasing my forehead. I knew I wasn't the only one troubled by the newspaper's report of the incident, because a nearly identical frown had created a furrow in Max's brow as well.

"They didn't say anything about the children," I said, and he nodded.

"Yeah, I noticed that, too. Do you think maybe the reporter left that part out because it concerned minors?"

I would have liked to think the man who'd written the article was only being discreet, but considering what I'd heard in my high school history classes about the sensational "yellow" journalism of the late nineteenth and early twentieth centuries, I didn't find that theory very likely.

"Maybe," I said. "But I think there's something else going on here." I got up from my chair and went over to where Dorothy had seated herself behind her desk. Max followed, expression curious. Directing my next words to her, I said, "We noticed there wasn't any mention of children in the newspaper article about the explosion. I thought those two kids whose ghosts are sometimes spotted in the Plaza Hotel died in the blast."

Dorothy lifted one eyebrow and smiled very faintly, as if amused that I was naïve enough to believe in those ghost tales. "Oh, no—I'm afraid you've got the story wrong. It's actually very tragic. Two of Antonio Moreno's grandchildren disappeared around that same time and were never seen again. The rumor was that they'd been taken by a group of vagrants who had a camp on the edge of town, but the local authorities and some of the townspeople went out and broke up the camp, and no trace of the children was ever found."

That piece of information made Max send me a sideways glance, one that told me he didn't believe the story for a second. "And no one thought it was a little convenient that the two kids vanished into thin air at the same time the boiler exploded?" he asked.

Apparently, Dorothy didn't care much for

Max's tone, because she drew herself up in her chair and gave him a very stern look. "I'm afraid you don't have all the facts, Mr. Sullivan. Believe me, an extensive investigation of the explosion was performed, and there definitely weren't any remains down there except those of Mr. Moreno."

Antonio Moreno, who I guessed must have been Leila's great-great-grandfather. Had the two children who'd disappeared been his son's kids, or had they belonged to one of his daughters?

In the end, I supposed it didn't matter who the children's parents had been. The little boy and girl were gone, but their ghosts still lingered at the Plaza Hotel, for whatever reason. Under other circumstances, I might have thought they hung around there because it was a place of happy memories for them, but I couldn't forget the way the girl had hung back, had acted as though she didn't want to go up those steps and into the hotel.

"Do you know their names?" I asked abruptly. "The boy and girl who disappeared, I mean."

Dorothy reached up with one hand to straighten her glasses. Judging by the look she'd just sent in my direction, I got the feeling she was wondering why all this should be so important to me.

And honestly, I wasn't sure why, except it seemed as if we were sitting on another mystery just as confounding as the circumstances of Calum's death, and my gut was telling me the two were related.

Even if I couldn't begin to say how...or why.

"Miguel was the little boy, and Ana was the little girl," Dorothy told me, and I couldn't quite hold back a ripple of excitement.

Ana Moreno. A.M.

Then again, her grandfather had been Antonio, also A.M.

Who had scratched those initials into the basement wall? During Max's and my brief encounter with the ghost girl the night before, I'd gotten the impression they were hers, but maybe she was only pointing at them because she wanted us to know her initials were A.M. as well.

This whole thing was making my head hurt.

"Do you need anything else?" Dorothy went on. "It's almost four, and I need to put things away so I can close on time."

And her gaze went past Max and me to the scatter of newspaper clippings we'd left on the table.

"No, that's all," I said hastily. Because Max didn't protest, I had to believe he also agreed that we'd learned pretty much everything we were going to—well, unless we came back and did some in-depth research.

In fact, he went over to the table and gathered

up the clippings, carefully sorting them and then paper-clipping them back together.

Looking somewhat mollified, Dorothy took the folder from him when he handed it over, and said, "If you think of anything else you want to look up, just let me know."

We thanked her and headed outside into the blazing heat. "I need a drink," Max said, a sentiment I totally agreed with.

"Sounds good," I replied. "But let's go to The Skillet instead of the Plaza."

"Don't want to bump into any ghosts?" he asked with a grin.

I didn't smile, though. For whatever reason, going over and having a drink at Byron T's sounded like a very bad idea right then. "Change of scenery," was all I said, but that seemed to be enough for Max.

"Coming right up. Your chariot awaits, milady."

He opened the Bronco's passenger-side door for me, and I got in. A minute later, the A/C was blasting and we were pulling away from the curb, leaving the historical society building...and any other secrets it might contain...behind.

We'd learned a few things, but way too many questions remained.

CHAPTER 15

Welcome to My Nightmare

A plate of curly fries and a hefeweizen helped my mood immensely, even though I couldn't escape the feeling that Max and I had both overlooked something important.

"Do you really buy that story about the camp full of vagrants?" he asked, and I shook my head.

"No," I replied, and sipped some more beer. "Or at least, I think those kinds of encampments weren't uncommon back then, but I also don't think they took the kids. Mostly, people like that just wanted to be left alone. They definitely wouldn't try to stir up trouble with the locals."

"That's what I was thinking." Max paused there to have a swallow of his own beer, also a hefeweizen. Honestly, it was too hot to drink much of anything else.

We'd gotten the booth up near the front

window, a choice spot that had only been available because it wasn't quite happy hour yet, and a lot of people were still at work. The air conditioning blasted away in the background, barely keeping up with the heat.

But it still felt good to be here, in a spot that felt like neutral territory. Although I'd certainly never had any ghost sightings on the main floor of the Plaza, I figured it was still better to be someplace else.

At that particular moment, I didn't think I could deal with any more spirits.

"So...what, then?" Max asked next. "You think the kids really were in the basement, and the management at the hotel covered it up for some reason?"

"Maybe," I said. "I don't know why, though."

He picked up a fry and munched on it in a contemplative sort of way, then washed it down with more beer. "I suppose it's possible that Antonio Moreno was bringing his grandkids to work with him when he wasn't supposed to, and then the hotel management lied about them not being down there when the boiler exploded. It would have looked bad, like they weren't paying attention to what their employees were doing when they were working with sensitive equipment."

That theory sounded plausible enough. I couldn't remember which year Byron T. Wells died, but even if he wasn't still alive and managing the place when the boiler accident occurred, the Plaza Hotel had been one of Las Vegas's most important institutions back then. Its owners might have done what they could to cover up any possible negligence, especially if it might have provided ammunition for a wrongful death lawsuit brought by the family against the hotel's owners.

If they even had wrongful death suits back then. I had to admit I wasn't exactly an expert when it came to historical jurisprudence.

But something was tickling at the back of my mind, telling me that wasn't what was going on here. Unfortunately, since I wasn't psychic or clairvoyant, I couldn't pull the answer out of thin air. No, about the only thing I could do was keep muddling along and hope that sooner or later, the truth would decide to reveal itself.

"You're not looking very convinced," Max remarked, and I sent him a rueful smile.

"I don't think I am convinced," I replied. "Not because I know anything for sure, but just because all this feels wrong."

"Maybe it's time for you to brew some more tea, see what the leaves have to say."

That actually sounded like a very good idea. There had been a couple of occasions when they'd steered me wrong, but mostly, the clues they provided were useful, even if sometimes it took me a while to figure out what they were trying to tell me.

"Yes, I probably should do that," I said. "And that means I'll need to go home."

At once, Max's expression turned wary. "Are you really sure you want to go back to your house after someone broke in there?"

Well, no, I really didn't, even if I didn't think we could technically call it "breaking in" when all the signs pointed to someone walking through an unlocked door.

But....

"All my tea-leaf reading supplies are there," I pointed out. "Also—and don't take this the wrong way—I need to be someplace I vibe with. I love your house, but it's not the same as being at my own home. I'll be totally fine."

For a moment, he was quiet, obviously studying my expression and trying to decide whether it was worth it to argue with me.

It seemed I looked sufficiently mulish, because he released a sigh and said, "Okay, if you have to."

"I do," I said. "But we'll need to go back to your place first so I can get my stuff."

He didn't look exactly thrilled by that prospect, although he didn't argue. Instead, his shoulders lifted, and he said, "Sure. No problem."

It felt strange to be back in my house, even though I'd only spent one night away. To be honest, that night at Max's house was the first time I hadn't slept in my own bed for more years than I could count. A world explorer, I was not.

But everything was quiet on the home front, and it seemed pretty clear to me nothing had been touched in my absence. Then again, why would it? My burglar had already retrieved the one thing he wanted.

Max had admonished me to keep everything locked up tight, a warning that only made me grin, considering how hot it was and how I'd obviously need to keep all the doors and windows shut to keep the cold air from the HVAC system inside.

Even so, I walked in and out of every room, making sure the windows were locked, eyeing every surface for signs someone else might have been in here during the twenty-four hours or so that I'd been gone.

There were none, of course. I put my overnight bag on the floor next to my bed and went back downstairs, knowing I needed to get some water boiling if this tea-leaf reading was going to happen any time this afternoon.

After I filled the kettle and set it on the stove, though, I couldn't help but let out a sigh. I really wished I could have stayed with Max rather than come back here, even if I understood why I needed to do this. We'd left the rest of the evening open-ended, since I wasn't sure how the reading was going to go. It would have been nice to think we'd meet for dinner after this, but I'd told him he shouldn't count on it.

He'd been disappointed...but he also hadn't pressed me. No, he'd just said to call him and check in, and maybe I'd be able to come over to his place for a barbecue the next night.

That prospect would have sounded a lot more enticing if I hadn't known Mason Fowles was hanging out in Max's casita, although I doubted Max would have given the guy an invitation to join us for burgers or tri-tip or whatever he thought he might make for dinner. Still, the place didn't feel as private as it once had, even though I understood Max and I were never truly alone there, thanks to either Al or Lou being on duty all the time to make sure the ranch was as secure as it could be.

The kettle began to whistle, so I turned it off and left it to cool while I got down my cup and saucer from the cupboard, along with the little tin of gunpowder green tea.

Maybe I should have selected something a little less explosive, considering I'd be asking about that damn boiler blast.

Too late now, though, since I'd already knocked a teaspoon of the loose tea into the cup. I went ahead and picked up the kettle, and poured water over the leaves before carrying the teacup and its matching flower-painted saucer over to the kitchen table.

For a moment, I sat there quietly, letting myself relax, letting all the worries and doubts of the past few days fade away. I couldn't claim that they were totally gone, but at least they'd been pushed to the back of my mind, allowing space for the all-important question to float to the surface.

What really happened to Ana Moreno?

I honestly couldn't say why the little girl was uppermost in my mind, since it sure sounded as though both she and her brother had died at the same time. Maybe it was only that I'd seen her face the night before, had done my best to communicate with her.

With that question fixed in my head, I drank the tea, draining the cup until there was only a bit of liquid left in the bottom. As usual, I upended the cup to let the last little dribbles of tea drip onto the saucer, and then turned it right-side up so I could see what the leaves had to say.

Just like the last time, there was that odd little line of leaf fragments along the middle of the teacup, looking for all the world like a thick chain.

Why the chain? Had Ana been confined to the basement, maybe as a sort of punishment?

The leaves weren't usually that literal, but I really didn't know what else to think.

I let out a breath, then got up from my seat so I could wash out the teacup and set it on a cloth on the counter to dry. As far as I could tell, I hadn't learned anything new. It was possible the leaves thought I had all the facts in hand, but I wasn't sure I believed that.

Right then, I really wasn't sure what to believe.

I'd slung my purse over the back of one of the kitchen chairs, so it only took me a minute to pull out my phone and send Max a quick text.

I tried the tea leaves and got the same chain shape, so I'm not sure what to do next.

He must have been waiting to hear from me, because his answer came back right away.

Do you want me to come over? We could order in and watch TV and chill out.

All that sounded really tempting...especially the "chill out" part, which I knew was shorthand for losing ourselves in my bedroom for a couple of hours. Maybe it would be better for me to take my mind off all this for a while.

But then I thought of Calum McRae, dead long before his time, and the sad face of the little girl I knew must be Ana Moreno. Didn't I owe it to those two souls to try my hardest to find out exactly what had happened to both of them?

That seemed to decide it. Max would under-stand...or at least, I hoped he would.

Wish I could.

I paused there, as a sudden thought came to me. Yes, my grandmother had warned me not to do this sort of thing again, but desperate times led to desperate measures.

I just thought of something I want to try. I'll keep you posted.

After sending the message, I set down my phone and glanced out the window. It might have still been bright afternoon, but I needed to attempt something dark.

Time to try a séance.

***

I closed all the drapes and blinds, and then lit three white pillar candles and set them on metal holders at the center of the dining room table. Maybe I couldn't even call this a real séance, not when it was just me reaching out to the world of the spirits and not a group of people pooling their energy to contact the ethereal plane—or whatever you wanted to call it—but it still seemed a good idea to me to use some of the trappings of a séance, no matter what exactly I was doing.

Once I had the downstairs prepared, I sat at the table and clasped my hands in front of me. A deep breath, during which I reassured myself that I'd spoken with my grandmother on another plane and therefore had done something like this before, although the circumstances were completely different.

Unlike before, though, I wasn't trying to reach out to the spirit of someone newly dead. I'd flirted with the idea of attempting to contact Calum first, but I remembered how it supposedly wasn't a good idea to try contacting someone who was new to the world of the spirits and figured it was probably better to try something a little safer.

Besides, something in my gut told me Ana Moreno and her brother were at the center of the mystery, even if they'd died a century before.

Just like when I'd tried to contact Tom Gallegos, the former mayor of Las Vegas, I closed my eyes and visualized a beautiful glade of trees all decked out in fresh spring green, with new grass under my feet. This time, I also imagined beds of daisies, cheerful and bright among the leaves of grass, and the chirping of birds overhead. A soft breeze caught my hair and whispered among the branches.

I hoped it would be enough.

"Ana!" I called out. "Ana Moreno!"

No response, although a finch flew out of the tree above me and glided down to peck at something in the grass.

Well, at least this little bubble on the astral plane was pretty realistic.

And I also knew that sometimes it took a while

for spirits to respond to your call. I had to imagine that a ghost's time sense wasn't the same as mine, that they'd long ago ceased to worry about the hours and minutes ticking past.

Maybe so. I was only glad that I'd fortified myself for this ordeal with a beer and some fries, just in case I ended up sitting here for longer than I'd planned.

But then I caught a glimpse of something moving in the trees on the other side of the glade, something small.

She came out into the clearing, dark hair shimmering in the sunlight. Now that she looked as real as I did, I could see her dress really was white with pink smocking, how her black kidskin Mary Jane–style shoes had been carefully polished to hide some of the wear on the toes.

As I watched, she came closer, her big brown eyes curious. Did she know she was dead? Could she somehow understand that I wasn't like her, that I was only a temporary visitor from the land of the living?

Since I hadn't been trained in any of this, it was really hard for me to say.

I smiled at her, though, and said, "Hello, Ana."

She tilted her small chin up at me, eyes narrowing slight. "*Hola. ¿Quién eres?*"

Oh, boy. I'd never even stopped to think that she didn't speak English. Or maybe she did, but was more comfortable in the Spanish that probably had been spoken in her home.

Time to dig up those long-forgotten phrases from my high school Spanish classes and hope like hell that I wouldn't mangle them too badly.

"*Mi español no es tan bueno. ¿Puede hablar Inglés?*"

She stared at me for a moment as she played with one of the long, sooty sausage curls that lay against the white and pink bodice of her dress. "A little."

Oh, thank God. No, we probably wouldn't be able to stand there and discuss the futility of existence or whatever, but I doubted a six- or seven-year-old like her would have been capable of such a thing even in the Spanish she was used to.

"Are you Ana Moreno?"

She nodded, curls bouncing.

Okay, at least I was able to confirm that much. "Do you have a brother named Miguel?"

Another nod, although her mouth drooped a little, as if signaling that the sound of her brother's name saddened her in some way.

"Is he here?" I asked next, and gestured toward the glade where we stood. About all I could do was hope she'd understand that I was asking about the astral plane in general, and not simply this little bubble of beauty I'd created as a venue for our conversation.

Now she shook her head, and her big brown eyes shimmered with tears. "No. He went to—went to—" She stopped there, frowning fiercely, as though she was trying her best to work out how to say it in English. After a moment, she pointed upward, saying, "He go to that place."

Was she trying to tell me her brother was in heaven? And if he was there, why hadn't she gone with him?

"You didn't go with him to heaven, too?"

Her fingers knotted in the full skirt of her dress, wrinkling the light cotton. "No. I can't go. Too...too...." She seemed to give up on English as she completed the sentence with, "*enojada.*"

What the heck did *enojada* mean? I wracked my brain, telling it to get its act together so I could remember all those long lists of vocabulary words from Ms. Sanchez's Spanish 1 class. It sounded so familiar....

Right. "*Enojada*" meant angry.

But Ana didn't look particularly angry. No, she looked more sad than anything else.

However, since she'd told me that much, I knew I needed to go on.

"Why angry?"

She stared down at the carefully polished but still scuffed toes of her Mary Janes. "No say."

"You can't say...or you don't want to?"

Again, her fingers knotted in the skirt of her dress, and her eyes wouldn't meet mine.

"I had a dream," I said, speaking slowly in the hope that she'd be able to understand what I was saying. "You know what that is?"

Slowly, she nodded, although she continued to look at the toes of her shoes as though they were the most fascinating things in the world. "When you are...are...*dormiendo.*"

"Right, when you're sleeping," I replied, and hoped my tone was soft and reassuring enough that she'd continue talking to me. "I saw you in my dream. You were walking up the steps to the Plaza Hotel—you know, the hotel *centro?*"

Thank God that bits and pieces of Spanish were coming back to me, even though I doubted I'd be able to string an entire sentence together.

Another nod, although her little rosebud of a mouth tightened, and I got the distinct impression she didn't want to talk about the place.

Unfortunately, I had to ask if I was ever going to get to the bottom of this.

"You were there with your brother and an older man. Was the man Antonio Moreno, your *abuelo?*"

She pulled in a breath and didn't reply. Now instead of looking at her shoes, she seemed fascinated by a patch of daisies growing only a few yards from where we stood.

Then she looked up at last, her dark eyes burning with rage. "He was a bad man."

Well, there was that anger she'd mentioned a few minutes earlier. And if she thought her grandfather was bad, then that definitely explained her obvious reluctance in my dream, the way she'd been trying to resist the hand that held hers.

"Bad," she repeated. "We went to the hotel *centro* with him. Miguel and me. Too many times. It was bad. He was bad."

Tears glittered in her eyes, and I wished I could reach out and give her a reassuring hug. Problem was, as real as she looked right now, she was still a ghost, a spirit, nothing more than photons using her will and her rage to give them shape and form. If I hugged her now, she'd evaporate into nothingness again.

Or at least, I thought that was how it was supposed to work.

I hated to ask the question, but I also knew I couldn't stop here. Not when I was finally starting to get some answers. "Bad...how?"

She shook her head, curls bouncing. "*No puedo decírtelo.*"

That one took me a few seconds.

I can't tell you.

"Did someone tell you not to talk about it?" I asked gently. A horrible churning in my gut told me what her secret probably was, and yet I needed more than terrible suspicions.

"*Sí, sí,*" she said. "*Mi abuela...mi madre.*"

Dear God. Her mother and grandmother had known, and had done nothing to stop it?

I had to remind myself it was a different time, a time when women had very little power of their own and when those sorts of accusations could destroy a family forever.

Not that they hadn't already destroyed Ana's life...and the life of her brother Miguel.

"Were you...." I paused to hunt for the words and realized I had absolutely no idea how to say "explode" in Spanish. "Were you and Miguel at the hotel when the boiler blew up?"

Her face contorted, and she gave a violent shake of her head. Not, I guessed, to indicate "no," but as if to knock the terrible memory right out of her brain.

And then she ran toward me, passed through me, and I saw. Only a flash, nothing compared to what that poor child had endured, but that one awful glimpse was enough.

Her grandfather had taken Ana and Miguel down to the basement near the boiler room and abused them. Ana much more often than Miguel, but neither child escaped the monster's attentions. They'd all been there when the boiler exploded, with Antonio far too preoccupied to realize the valve was about to fail and the boiler reach critical mass.

Miguel somehow had managed to deal with his trauma and move on. Ana, however, had not.

But if Miguel was in heaven, why was his ghost sometimes still seen at the Plaza Hotel? Did he return from time to time to try to help his sister move on?

I didn't know. There was still so much I didn't know.

The glade around me faded, and I was back in my dining room, sitting there and staring at the white candles in the center of the table.

What should I do now?

My thoughts were racing all over the place, and my hands shook. I got up from my chair and leaned over so I could blow out the candles. Then I went to the windows and opened the curtains one by one, letting in a flood of afternoon light.

I needed that light to chase away the darkness I'd just seen.

And now that the light was on, I had to figure out what to do next.

CHAPTER 16

Chain of Fools

"They all must have covered it up," Max said.

We were sitting in my living room and drinking iced tea, mostly because my nerves were already shot and I knew that having any kind of alcohol probably wasn't a very good idea. I'd also debated with myself as to whether I should even have Max come over, but then realized it was stupid to struggle through this alone when he was there, waiting and willing to offer me any comfort I might need.

"That's what I was thinking," I replied, then put my tea back down on its coaster. "The people in this town would rather have pretended that those poor kids were kidnapped by vagrants than admit one of their own could have committed such heinous crimes."

Max rubbed a thoughtful hand over his chin.

"Well, sometimes people have a hard time acknowledging things that shatter their worldview, or admitting they might have been complicit in those kinds of terrible acts. I mean, if Antonio was bringing those kids with him to work on a regular basis, you'd think someone would have wondered if something fishy was going on."

One would think. And the truly awful thing was that I had absolutely no idea what I should do next, and I guessed Max didn't, either. After all, anyone who'd been involved in that cover-up must have been dead for decades, so what would we be proving by making the facts of the case public now?

Not that we had any actual facts to present. I guessed most people in town wouldn't exactly believe me if I told them I'd had a convo with Ana Moreno's ghost, my expertise with tea leaves notwithstanding.

Since I didn't know what to say and only sat there in brooding silence, Max clearly felt compelled to speak again.

"But now that we know about Ana and her brother, that they died there, is there anything we can do to help them move on?"

I tilted my head at him, even as I wondered what the heck he was suggesting. "I'm no ghost-whisperer, Max."

He smiled, a smile that wasn't quite as incandescent as usual, probably because of the sober subject matter we were discussing. "I think some people might disagree, considering how you got Ana to open up to you. But that's not what I meant. I mean, I assume she and her brother were Catholic, so maybe we could try having a local priest come down there and bless the space, maybe conduct some kind of funeral mass so they know it's okay to leave this plane?"

His tone was hesitant, as if he wasn't quite sure whether his suggestion had any merit at all. I leaned over and kissed him on the cheek, heartened by his concern for those souls who had left this world so violently and far, far too soon.

"I get the feeling Miguel mostly isn't here," I said. "That's probably why he isn't spotted nearly as much as Ana is. But yes, that sounds like a good idea. She needs to know that she was finally able to tell someone the truth, and there's no reason for her to remain here."

"And the priest needs to know the service would only be for Ana and Miguel," Max added, his voice hardening. "That bastard Antonio's spirit can rot in that basement for all eternity, as far as I'm concerned.

Since I wholeheartedly agreed with that particular sentiment, I didn't even try to argue. Was Antonio even aware that the spirits of his two grandchildren still haunted the hotel, or did they all exist on separate levels of the afterlife? It sounded as though Miguel came and went as he pleased, while Ana was definitely stuck here. And while Antonio was spotted from time to time, it also didn't seem as though he appeared as often as Ana.

Well, if Max and I had anything to do with it, she wouldn't be caught there, a delicate butterfly in amber, for much longer.

But even though I'd uncovered an admittedly sordid piece of the puzzle, it didn't seem as if I was any closer to finding out who or what had frightened Calum to death. There had to be a connection, but what? Had Antonio's ghost appeared in Calum's room and threatened him somehow, maybe fearing that Calum was about to stumble across his terrible secret?

I told Max I wasn't sure I'd really done all that much, and while he didn't shrug, I could tell by the way he leaned over and gave my hand a reassuring squeeze that he was sure I'd figure it out eventually.

"You did something really major today, you know," he said. "I think it's okay to give yourself a little break."

He was probably right, even though my mind couldn't quite let it go. If nothing else, the actual anniversary of the boiler explosion was coming up in just two days. What if Ana had something particularly spectacular planned for that gruesome commemoration?

I didn't voice those doubts to Max, mostly because I wanted to believe I was borrowing trouble. Yes, the ghosts had been a little more active lately, but nothing too terrible had happened...well, unless you counted all those issues with the elevator, and I still didn't even know for sure whether the Plaza Hotel's ghosts had been responsible for the glitches, or whether those problems had purely mechanical origins.

Instead, I agreed when Max suggested getting some takeout, and was able to relax somewhat as we ate our tacos and then spent the rest of the evening snuggled up against each other on the couch, my head pillowed on his shoulder as we started to get caught up on the latest season of *The Mandalorian*. He somehow sensed this was the kind of intimacy I wanted, and didn't push things beyond that.

It felt so real, so comfortable, this quiet time we spent together.

All I could do was hope it would go on forever.

———

That Friday, I was less inclined to go in to work than ever, although I told myself at least I would have the weekend to rest and recover. Also, Deanne was getting back late Sunday, and although I'd told her to take Monday off, she'd insisted on being at Levitation Latte when she was supposed to, if maybe not right at the crack of dawn.

And that was fine. I could open the shop by myself, but just knowing she'd be at work to spell me so I wouldn't have to carry the entire load on my own made a world of difference in my mind.

Max and I had decided to keep our findings to ourselves until we had something more concrete to go on, so I did my best to act as though I hadn't heard those terrible revelations from Ana the night before, that I hadn't discovered something dark and seamy in our quiet little town. A few of my customers made sideways comments that let me know they were all too aware of how Max Sullivan and Skye O'Malley were now an item, but I just wore my best customer-service smile and tried not to give away any details.

After all, this was my personal life, not theirs.

At around two, Leila came in for her ritual early afternoon green iced tea pick-me-up. As usual, she was wearing the button-down black shirt and black pants her position at the Plaza Hotel's bar required, but because it was so darn hot—I was sure we would break a few records today—she had the long sleeves rolled way up, exposing most of her upper arms.

Around her left bicep was a tattoo of a chain.

My eyes widened. Was that the chain the tea leaves had been trying to tell me about?

And here I'd thought they did their best to avoid being too literal.

Then I realized I was staring, and blinked. "Hi, Leila," I said, praying to God I sounded completely natural. "Some iced tea?"

"Yes, please," she said. "I can't believe how frigging hot it is out there."

"It's definitely nasty," I said. "Let me get you your drink."

I turned away, mind working furiously. The chain must have been a recent addition, because I knew Leila didn't have it last summer, and I didn't think I'd seen it as recently as a month ago, when I'd bumped into her at Walmart just as the weather started to turn warm. She'd been wearing a sleeveless shirt with a Western-style cross on the front, and I hadn't seen any tattoo on her arm then.

Well, not a chain tattoo. She already had the Zia sunburst—New Mexico's state symbol—inked on her other arm, but it seemed she'd recently decided she needed to add something more.

So...were the leaves trying to tell me that Leila had something to do with Calum's death?

A sinking sensation in my stomach told me I had to believe that, even as I couldn't quite understand how pretty, bubbly Leila Moreno could have possibly done anything that would have caused

Calum to expire of fright. She couldn't look threatening if she tried.

That chain tattoo couldn't be a coincidence, though. No way.

I finished filling her go-cup with iced tea and handed it back over to her. She gave me several dollar bills in exchange, then added, "Is everything okay? You look kind of weird."

So much for my poker face. "Oh, I'm fine," I said hastily. "I think the heat's just starting to get to me. We need some monsoon storms to come in here and cool things down."

A shrug, followed by, "Well, I heard there might be more tomorrow, so just hang in there."

She raised her cup of tea in what might have been a gesture of thanks or just a simple goodbye, then headed out. For a second, I stood behind the counter, not sure what to do. Part of me wanted to run after her and accuse her right then and there of killing Calum McRae.

Reason prevailed, though, and I remained where I was. For one thing, it was pushing a hundred outside, and I didn't want to have that kind of confrontation while risking keeling over from heat prostration. Also, this was one time I definitely didn't want to face down a killer on my own.

No, I needed to have Max with me.

The situation was so important that I'd called him rather than sending a text, and he agreed to meet me at my house as soon as I got off work. In fact, he was so ready to confront Leila that he was sitting at the curb in his Bronco when I drove up.

"What time does she get off work?" he asked after we'd sat down in the living room with some ice water and freshly cut lemon slices from the tree in my yard.

"On Fridays? Usually around eight or nine, depending on when she came in."

"So if we go to her house around nine-thirty, she should be there," Max said.

I gave an uncertain lift of my shoulders. "Maybe...unless she decides to go out. It *is* Friday night, after all."

"Even if she does, there aren't that many places she could go," he replied, looking as unconcerned as only Max Sullivan could. "We'll track her down."

He was right about that—it wasn't as though Las Vegas boasted dozens of nightclubs or anything. But still, there was always a chance Leila would head to a party at someone's house rather than deciding to have a beer at The Skillet or listen to whichever band was playing that night at Black-

CHRISTINE POPE

ie's, down on the I-25 frontage road a mile or so from where Max and I were currently sitting.

Even if we did find her, I really didn't like the idea of having this conversation in public. It was going to be hard enough in the privacy of the little house she was renting a few streets over from mine.

"Well, we'll try her house first," I said. "If she's not there...then we'll see what happens."

"Okay." Max was silent for a moment, obviously turning over scenarios in his head. "I have to wonder what set her off. I mean, Leila Moreno seems like the last person who would ever resort to violence."

"I know," I responded, since I'd thought the same thing at least a dozen times since I spotted that chain tattoo on her arm a few hours earlier. "But the tea leaves were pretty clear, so I know we need to talk to her. If I've made a horrible mistake, well, I'll apologize."

Exactly how I was supposed to apologize for accusing someone of murder, I didn't know, but I hoped I would figure it out somehow.

Because Max and I had hours to use up before Leila would be off work, we decided to get a bite to eat at The Skillet and then come back and watch some TV. I doubted I'd remember a single plot point of whatever we watched, but at least it was a way to kill some time.

We were alone, too, because once Tilly found

out Max was coming over, she'd put down her little black paw and told me she definitely was going to tough it out on her own this weekend.

"Just put out enough food to get me through to Sunday," she said, sounding annoyed. "I refuse to be at your house with those sorts of activities going on over my head."

I hadn't argued, partly because we'd already agreed that Tilly could stay away if she wanted to, and partly because I had enough on my plate without worrying about the cat as well. Seriously, though, I doubted Tilly had to worry about those kinds of "activities" happening before the mystery was resolved. I loved Max, and I loved being with him, but romance was definitely not in the air at the moment.

He seemed to understand, because he hadn't even suggested that we might occupy ourselves upstairs in the bedroom rather than downstairs in front of the TV. No, he just sat there with me, his hand clasped in mine, while we watched old episodes of *Is It Cake* that we'd missed, and did our best not to have our eyes glued to the clock on the mantel.

Eventually, nine-thirty rolled around, and the two of us got up from the sofa and headed out so we could walk over to Leila's place. Even at that hour, the heat hadn't faded completely, although at least it had dropped from nearly the century mark to somewhere much more comfortable, probably in the low eighties.

We held hands as we walked, although neither of us said anything. It could have been because it was late enough that we didn't want to attract too much attention or—much more likely—that we simply wanted to save our energy for what we both knew was going to be an extremely uncomfortable conversation.

I probably should have been relieved to see Leila's old Toyota truck in the driveway and a light on in the front room. The coward in me, though, only thought it might have been nice to have her working late or out somewhere, anything that might have delayed this confrontation.

Max's hand in mine gave me the strength I needed, though, and that was why I was able to walk up the path that led to her front door with my head held high and my heart beating at a somewhat normal rhythm. Still with his fingers clasped in mine, he reached out to ring the doorbell with his free hand.

A long pause, during which I wondered if she wasn't going to answer. Maybe she was thinking this was a crazy time for someone to drop by unannounced, and I had to agree with her on that.

But then the door opened, and she blinked out at us, clearly shocked to see a movie star and the local coffee shop owner standing on her doorstep at nine-thirty on a Friday night.

"Skye?" she said, tone so questioning, it sounded as if she wasn't even sure whether that was my name.

"Hi, Leila," I replied, doing my best to sound completely casual. "Max and I wanted to talk to you about something."

A long pause, during which she continued to stare at us. Her expression shifted, though, moving from shock to something that looked like outright fear.

"I was just getting ready for bed—" she said, and began to close the door.

However, Max reached out and caught it before it had shut more than an inch or so. "This won't take very long."

His tone was firm, the kind of voice I'd heard him use in movies where he played a cop or a government agent. It worked in those films, and it seemed to be effective now as well, because Leila's shoulders slumped and she stepped out of the way.

"All right," she said in barely more than a mumble.

Not exactly the most congenial welcome in the world, but that was fine. The important thing was that she hadn't slammed the door in our faces.

Her rented house wasn't very big, just a small living room with an eating area to one side, open to the postage-stamp kitchen. It had been decorated with a mishmash of hand-me-down furniture or maybe stuff she'd bought at garage sales, because nothing really seemed to go with anything else... and not in a charming, boho sort of way, either.

She picked up a plastic laundry basket from one end of the threadbare couch and said, "You can sit down if you want."

Max and I looked at each other, and he shook his head ever so slightly.

"No, that's okay," I said. "This won't take long."

Her dark eyes met mine, wide and wary, like a deer that had just seen an oncoming semi as it began to cross a highway. "And what exactly is 'this'?"

Max spoke then, tone gentler than I'd expected. "I think you know, Leila. Do you want to tell us about what happened to Calum McRae?"

Her response was immediate, although her voice sounded shaky. "I don't know anything more than you do."

"Really?" I asked. "Because I think you needed to stop him from writing his book when he found out about what your great-great-grandfather was doing to those two kids."

Leila's face crumpled then, like a piece of delicate origami that had been crushed by a careless fist. "We didn't mean for that to happen," she whispered. "We just wanted him to go away so he wouldn't say anything."

Once again, Max and I looked at each other. "'We'?" I repeated.

Leila stared down at the floor. Her long, dark hair swung forward, but it wasn't quite enough to obscure the tears that had begun to flow down her cheeks. "I got Pedro to help me. I knew he had a thing for me, so it was easy to convince him that all I wanted was to scare Calum away."

So much for my instincts about people. Never in a million years would I have thought Pedro Montaño would be caught up in all this.

Max spoke up then. "Scare Calum how?"

Leila rubbed her hands against the thighs of her faded jeans, as if doing so could somehow wipe away the stain of the terrible thing she'd done. "Remember how I used to do makeup for the drama club in high school?"

I nodded at once, while Max only tilted his head ever so slightly, expression puzzled. His response made sense, since he'd been a year ahead of me in school, while Leila was two years younger than I was. She'd only been a freshman when he graduated, and he probably didn't remember all that much about her.

"Anyway," she went on, "I made up Pedro to look all wasted away and pale, like a ghost, and he put on a black suit he'd bought for his grandfather's funeral. We wanted Calum to think he was Antonio's spirit or something, so we could frighten him into running away and hopefully leaving it behind."

"Leaving what behind?" Max asked her, looking more mystified than ever, even as I realized this was almost the exact scenario I'd imagined earlier that day.

Or at least, I'd imagined Antonio appearing to Calum and trying to frighten him off. Never in my wildest dreams had I thought Leila might somehow be involved.

"My *tía* Dolores's diary," Leila replied in answer to Max's question. "I didn't even know it existed until a few days ago, when my *tía* confessed to me that she'd given it to Calum, that she couldn't keep the family secret any longer."

"The secret about Antonio," I murmured, and Leila gave a dreary little nod.

"My great-great-grandmother gave her diary to her daughter Catalina before she passed, and Catalina gave it to her niece Dolores. And when Calum came to talk to *tía* Dolores, she decided he should be the one to tell the world what really happened."

Although I wanted to be furious with Leila for what she'd done to Calum, I couldn't ignore the ragged despair in her voice. "Because your great-

great-grandmother wrote the truth in that diary," I said quietly.

Leila reached up to wipe away some tears, sniffling as she nodded again. "Yes. I suppose she just couldn't keep it in and had to write it down somewhere. It was a terrible secret my family worked very hard to keep hidden, and when I found out what my *tía* had done, I knew I just couldn't let Calum McRae expose it and ruin all of us."

"That all happened a hundred years ago," I said, my tone gentler than I'd expected it to be. "Do you really think anyone would blame you for what your great-great-grandfather did?"

Her shoulders lifted. She was still wearing the black button-down shirt that was part of her bartender's uniform, although now the sleeves had been rolled down, concealing the tattoo that had been the one clue to lead us to this place. "People are funny that way," she said, her voice now flat, almost emotionless, as though she'd gone past caring about any of this now that the truth had come out. "They'd look at my family, talk about us behind our backs."

"So...you hoped to scare Calum off and have him take the diary with him, and never come back to Las Vegas," Max put in.

Leila let out a breath. "Yeah. Pedro already searched the room for it and couldn't find it, so we decided that scaring Calum away was the best thing to do. But after Pedro unlocked the door to his room and sneaked up behind him while he was working on his laptop, he slammed the thing closed, stared at Pedro in shock, and grabbed his chest."

I could practically see the scene now—Pedro letting himself in with the master key that was part of his job as the hotel's night manager, moving quietly behind Calum, who was probably so absorbed in whatever he was working on that he hadn't heard a thing. There was no way to know whether he'd shut the laptop as a reflex or whether he'd intentionally known to close it so its contents would be locked down tight, but either way, neither Leila nor Pedro would have been able to access its secrets.

"Pedro freaked out and ran and went into the bathroom to scrub his face and change his clothes," Leila went on. "And then you came about twenty minutes later, and I knew there wasn't anything I could do to keep you from finding Calum without making you suspicious."

Calum, who might still be alive if Pedro had kept his wits about him and stayed to administer CPR, call an ambulance. Anger boiled in me at Pedro's and Leila's carelessness, at the way they'd tried to do whatever they could to cover their own asses when fast medical intervention might have saved Calum's life.

Max must have been making the same mental calculations, because his voice was uncharacteristically cold as he said, "So, you let a man die rather than do the right thing."

Leila's mouth tightened. "We were scared, okay? We weren't thinking straight. And then after —well afterward, we just decided the best thing to do was keep quiet. We really thought everyone would think Calum had died of natural causes. We didn't think Chief DeVargas would go and arrest someone who had nothing to do with it."

"But she did," Max said, still in that flat, chilly tone. "Which means you have to go to the police and tell them the same thing you just told us. Otherwise, an innocent man might end up in prison."

At first, she only stared at him, face still so tight with worry, she was barely recognizable. Then her head drooped, and she said, "I know."

I glanced over at Max, and he nodded. "In fact," I said, "we'll drive you there."

CHAPTER 17
Lux Aeterna

The news swept over the town quickly, as I'd supposed it would. At the moment, Leila and Pedro were both sitting in jail, awaiting arraignment when the judge was back in his chambers on Monday morning.

"But I doubt they'll go for anything more than involuntary manslaughter," Max remarked. "I mean, the whole thing is a complete mess, but it's pretty obvious that Pedro and Leila never intended to do anything except frighten Calum off. They couldn't have known about his heart defect."

No, of course they couldn't, because Calum himself hadn't known about it, either.

The two of us had just gotten back from the police station. Darcy Montoya, who was working the front desk that Saturday morning, had called to let me know the deputies who'd searched Leila

Moreno's house had found Calum's missing laptop there. Because Kate McRae had told the police she was giving me the MacBook Air, they'd known to reach out to me to come retrieve it.

"Although you really should have reported it stolen," Darcy had told me, to which I'd only given a helpless shrug.

"It's okay," I said. "No harm, no foul."

She'd shaken her head but didn't make any other comments on the situation. Most likely, she'd guessed I was feeling foolish over the laptop being taken at all, and that was why I'd kept my mouth shut about its disappearance. Because yes, Leila had taken it, but only because I'd been stupid enough to leave my back door unlocked. If she'd come to the house and hadn't been able to get in, I had no doubt that the laptop would have remained safe in my desk drawer.

And now it was sitting on my coffee table, the little Apple logo on its silvery case looking almost accusing, as though it expected me to have done a much better job of freeing its secrets.

"I might as well send it back to Calum's sister," I said. "It's not as though I've had any luck with it."

Max reached over and pressed a soft kiss against my cheek. "Maybe not, but you still found the people responsible for his death, so I'd say that's a pretty big deal."

True...I supposed. All the same, I didn't like

that we might never figure out what he had written in there, or where he'd hidden Leila's great-great-grandmother's diary.

"In fact," Max went on, "I think we need to have a day of doing absolutely nothing. We can get takeout for lunch and come back here and completely veg out. Sound like a plan?"

I made a noncommittal noise. While part of me definitely liked the idea of sitting next to Max on the couch all day, I couldn't shake the feeling that we needed to be doing something more than that.

"Let's see what's on," he suggested, clearly undeterred by my lackluster response to his suggestion. He reached for the remote and turned on the TV.

Ironically, the television was tuned to a channel playing *Ghostbusters*. The screen showed their souped-up vintage station wagon, the Ecto I, screaming around a corner, sirens blaring.

It was as though someone had just smacked me upside the head, and I remembered how Calum had grinned when I'd trotted out that *Ghostbusters* quote during our very first meeting. "Oh, my God!" I blurted, and Max lifted an eyebrow.

"I can turn on something else if you want."

"No," I replied hastily. "This is fine. But I think I figured it out."

And as he stared at me with raised eyebrows, I reached for Calum's laptop, revealing the now all-too-familiar login screen with the little dialog box in the center.

As Max looked on, I typed in *Ectoplasm*.

And at once, the dialogue box disappeared and was replaced by a desktop displaying a gorgeous night-sky image of Monument Valley with the arc of the Milky Way overhead.

"Holy crap," Max breathed. "You did it."

"I don't think I would have ever figured it out if you hadn't turned that on," I said, and inclined my head toward the TV screen, where the Ghostbusters were now battling it out with a slimy poltergeist in the upper floors of a swanky Manhattan hotel. "I tried so many different combinations of words and numbers, but 'ectoplasm' never even entered my mind."

He took my hand and gave it a quick squeeze. "That's my girl. Let's see what you found."

Although I really didn't like the idea of poking around on Calum's computer, I knew it was necessary. Luckily, he had all his ghost-hunting files in one folder, with a bunch of subfolders labeled with the name of each location where he'd conducted a particular investigation.

Because everything was so organized, it wasn't too hard to find the "Las Vegas" folder. Inside it were several different documents and image files. A quick scan of the one titled "Notes" had Dolores Moreno's name and address, telling me Calum definitely had put the clues together and figured out she was the one person who might hold the key to the mystery of those ghostly children in the Plaza Hotel's basement.

There was also a cryptic note that had the Hotel Castañeda's phone number and address, along with "Room 114."

Max and I exchanged a puzzled glance. "Was Calum staying at the Castañeda, too?" he asked.

"Not that I'm aware of," I said. "I guess we'd better go check it out."

Maybe a simple phone call would have sufficed, but this somehow felt like something we needed to handle in person. The two of us got up from the couch and headed out into the blazing heat so we could climb into his Bronco and drive over to the Plaza's sister hotel.

The front desk clerk was helping an older couple when we entered the lobby, so Max and I had to hang back for a moment until their business was concluded. Once they'd walked away from the desk—and after the woman sent a single startled look in Max's direction, apparently realizing she was in the company of Hollywood royalty—we went up to the clerk.

I didn't recognize her, but that didn't matter. What mattered was whether or not she could tell us what was going on with Calum and Room 114.

"Hi," I said to the woman, who was blonde

and looked as though she was about five or six years older than I was. "A friend of mine had a room here —number 114. Did he leave anything there? His name was Calum McRae."

At once, her expression grew sober, as if she'd heard the story and knew the man who'd rented that room a few days ago was now gone. "I'm so sorry," she murmured. "But yes, he did. That is, he got the room so he'd be able to leave something here for you. Are you Skye O'Malley?"

I nodded, mystified, as she went over to the old-fashioned shelf behind her with its numerous cubbyholes, then pulled out a small, paper-wrapped volume.

Even as I took it, I knew exactly what Calum had left here for me.

María Moreno's diary.

Why he'd gone to these lengths to hide the little leather-bound volume, I didn't know for sure, but I had to believe he somehow knew the Plaza wasn't the best place to store it. Rather than go to the trouble of getting a local safety deposit box, he'd left the diary in a spot where it would be safe...but also where no one else would think to look.

"Thank you," I said. I didn't even know exactly what I would do with the thing—return it to Dolores Moreno, María Moreno's great-niece?— but at least now that last piece of the mystery had been tied up.

Or rather, one of those last pieces.

There was still one left.

It was an odd little group that gathered in the basement of the Plaza Hotel—Max and me, and Mason Fowles, who'd insisted on staying for the ceremony, a teary-eyed Dolores Moreno, and Father Salvador, the priest from the local Catholic church. When Max had first suggested that we should do our best to convince Ana it was time to move on and to give her a proper funeral, I'd thought it was kind of a silly idea.

But then I realized her spirit needed this closure, and I hoped it might give her the comfort and strength she needed. And when we explained to Father Salvador what we wanted to do, he'd agreed immediately.

That was why we were all here now. None of the other Morenos wanted to be present—for obvious reasons—but it seemed Dolores needed closure of her own after hiding such a terrible secret for so many years. She stood a little ways off from the rest of us, and wore a black lace scarf that covered her gray-streaked hair. When we'd met her at the entrance to the basement, she hadn't been able to meet any of our eyes, even though I'd made a point of thanking her for coming.

Father Salvador conducted most of the mass in Spanish, but as he came around to the end, he shifted to English, possibly because he wanted all of us there to understand what he was saying.

"Eternal rest, grant unto her, O Lord, and let perpetual light shine upon her. May she rest in peace. May her soul and the souls of all the faithful departed, through the mercy of God, rest in peace. Amen."

The rest of us murmured "amen" in response, and then we all fell silent again. Max's hand found mine, and I was glad of his reassuring touch, glad he was standing there next to me.

The priest closed his Bible, and I looked over at Dolores, whose head was bent. Behind the fall of her black lace veil, I thought I saw her lips moving.

And then brilliant white light flashed in the dim space, seeming to come from everywhere at once. Silhouetted against that diamond-hard illumination was what I thought looked like the shape of a young boy, his hand outstretched.

Yes, that was Miguel, reaching out to Ana, who emerged from the shadows to take her brother's hand. For just a moment, I could see the two of them standing there hand in hand, and then the light vanished, and we mere mortals were left to blink against the darkness left behind.

Father Salvador's thin, sensitive features were

suffused with pure joy. "She has gone," he said quietly. "She has gone home to God."

For a second, I couldn't say anything, could only gaze at the spot where the two ghosts had stood only a moment earlier.

Then Max leaned down and murmured, his hand still warm and comforting in mine, "It's time for us to go home, too."

We walked out of the basement, the rest of our little group trailing behind us.

Whatever happened after this, I knew that two of the Plaza Hotel's resident ghosts would never be seen again.

Max and Skye's adventures continue in *Sugar Skulls and Specters*.

Also by Christine Pope

FAMILIAR SPIRITS

(Cozy Mystery/Paranormal Romance)

Spells and Spaniels

Cauldrons and Cats

Hexes and Hedgehogs (November 2023)

LATTES AND LEVITATION

(Cozy Mystery/Paranormal Romance)

Caffeine Before Curses

Muffins After Magic

Pastries and Prophecies

Eclairs and Ectoplasm

Sugar Skulls and Specters (October 2023)

HEDGEWITCH FOR HIRE

(Cozy Mystery/Paranormal Romance)

Grave Mistake

Social Medium

Household Demons

Perpetual Potion

Jingle Spells

Wandering Monsters

Uninvited Ghosts

Prophet Motive

Ballroom Bits

Spell Check

———

UNEXPECTED MAGIC*

(Urban Fantasy/Paranormal Romance)

Found Objects

Finders, Keepers

Lost and Found

Finding Destiny

———

THE WITCHES OF WHEELER PARK*

(Paranormal Romance)

Storm Born

Thunder Road

Winds of Change

Mind Games

A Wheeler Park Christmas

Blood Ties

Healing Hands

Wishful Thinking

Smoke and Mirrors

———

MISS PRIMM'S ACADEMY FOR WAYWARD
WITCHES*

(Fantasy/Academy Romance)

Misspelled

Dispelled

Expelled

———

PROJECT DEMON HUNTERS*

(Paranormal Romance)

Unquiet Souls

Unbound Spirits

Unholy Ground

Unseen Voices

Unmarked Graves

Unbroken Vows

THE DEVIL YOU KNOW*

(Paranormal Romance)

Sympathy for the Devil

Charmed, I'm Sure

A Wing and a Prayer

Wish Upon a Star

THE WITCHES OF CANYON ROAD*

(Paranormal Romance)

Hidden Gifts

Darker Paths

Mysterious Ways

A Canyon Road Christmas

Demon Born

An Ill Wind

Higher Ground

Haunted Hearts

THE WITCHES OF CLEOPATRA HILL*

(Paranormal Romance)

Darkangel

Darknight

Darkmoon

Sympathetic Magic

Protector

Spellbound

A Cleopatra Hill Christmas

Impractical Magic

Strange Magic

The Arrangement

Defender

Bad Blood

Deep Magic

Darktide

THE DJINN WARS*

(Paranormal Romance)

Chosen

Taken

Fallen

Broken

Forsaken

Forbidden

Awoken

Illuminated

Stolen

Forgotten

Driven

Unspoken

THE WATCHERS TRILOGY*

(Paranormal Romance)

Falling Dark

Dead of Night

Rising Dawn

THE SEDONA FILES*

(Paranormal/Science Fiction Romance)

Bad Vibrations

Desert Hearts

Angel Fire

Star Crossed

Falling Angels

Enemy Mine

TALES OF THE LATTER KINGDOMS*

(Fantasy Romance)

All Fall Down

Dragon Rose

Binding Spell

Ashes of Roses

One Thousand Nights

Threads of Gold

The Wolf of Harrow Hall

Moon Dance

The Song of the Thrush

THE GAIAN CONSORTIUM SERIES*

(Science Fiction Romance)

Beast (free prequel novella)

Blood Will Tell

Breath of Life

The Gaia Gambit

The Mandala Maneuver

The Titan Trap

The Zhore Deception

The Refugee Ruse

STANDALONE TITLES

Hearts on Fire (Paranormal Romance)

Taking Dictation (Contemporary Romance)

Golden Heart (Gaslight Fantasy Romance)

Night Music: A Modern Reimagining of The Phantom
of the Opera (Contemporary Romance)

Ghost Dance: A Sequel to Gaston Leroux's The
Phantom of the Opera (Historical Mystery/Romance)

Flight Before Christmas (Fantasy Romance)

* Indicates a completed series

About the Author

USA Today bestselling author Christine Pope has been writing stories ever since she commandeered her family's Smith-Corona typewriter back in grade school. Her work includes paranormal romance, fantasy romance, and science fiction/space opera romance. She makes her home in beautiful Santa Fe, New Mexico.

Don't miss out on any of Christine's new releases —sign up for her newsletter today!

Christine Pope on the Web:
www.christinepope.com